Graduation night

On graduation night, I wore my beautiful white dress, and I *felt* beautiful, even with the knowledge of my nude-colored bra pressing into my shoulder blades. Mom had finally gotten around to hemming the one loose thready part, and she'd bought me a pair of white sandals with teeny blue dragonflies where the straps crossed over my toes. I wore my blue flower earrings and felt exquisite from head to toe.

"You look like a fairy," Dinah whispered as we lined up to the right of the stage.

"Don't I?" I replied. I grinned and sashayed my hips. Then I leaned in and said, "You look good, too. I really like your necklace."

"Thanks," she said, blushing. It was so easy to make her happy. It made me happy, making her happy. Tonight was all about being happy.

When the ceremony was over, we were sixth graders no more. We were soon-to-be seventh graders. Soon-to-be-junior highers. We shrieked with the weirdness of it while our parents chatted in the parking lot, and we ran like crazy around the playground. One last glorious free-for-all, like those funny square hats thrown into the sky. Only we were the ones flung topsy-turvy, not knowing where we would land.

OTHER BOOKS YOU MAY ENJOY

Twelve

Lauren Myracle

PUFFIN BOOKS

To all the girls who cheered for Winnie the first time around: this one's for you!

PUFFIN BOOKS
Published by the Penguin Group
Penguin Young Readers Group, 345 Hudson Street, New York, New York 10014, U.S.A.
Penguin Group (Canada), 90 Eglinton Avenue East, Suite 700,
Toronto, Ontario, Canada M4P 2Y3 (a division of Pearson Penguin Canada Inc.)
Penguin Books Ltd, 80 Strand, London WC2R 0RL, England
Penguin Ireland, 25 St Stephen's Green, Dublin 2, Ireland (a division of Penguin Books Ltd)
Penguin Group (Australia), 250 Camberwell Road, Camberwell, Victoria 3124, Australia
(a division of Pearson Australia Group Pty Ltd)
Penguin Books India Pvt Ltd, 11 Community Centre,
Panchsheel Park, New Delhi - 110 017, India
Penguin Group (NZ), 67 Apollo Drive, Rosedale, North Shore 0632, New Zealand
(a division of Pearson New Zealand Ltd)
Penguin Books (South Africa) (Pty) Ltd, 24 Sturdee Avenue,
Rosebank, Johannesburg 2196, South Africa

Registered Offices: Penguin Books Ltd, 80 Strand, London WC2R 0RL, England

First published in the United States of America by Dutton Children's Books,
a division of Penguin Young Readers Group, 2007
Published by Puffin Books, a division of Penguin Young Readers Group, 2008

5 7 9 10 8 6

Puffin Books ISBN 978-0-14-241091-2

Book design by Irene Vandervoort
Printed in the United States of America

Acknowledgments

Thanks to Trinity and Westminster for being such terrific schools;
I had a lot of fun within your hallowed halls.
Thanks to Rivendell for being the most wonderful school ever
for my own kids—we're all having oodles of fun in your halls,
even those of us way past sixth grade! Thanks especially to
Jane and Michele's class for the freewrite y'all did for me;
to Pam Iyer for her fabulous "Then and Now" presentations;
and to Seth Turner for introducing me to the world of hip-hop.

Thanks to Judy Blume for her fantastic books. They inspired me
then, and they inspire me now. Thanks to Mom, Dad, Susan
White, Laura Pritchett, and Cecil Castellucci for being early
readers, and thanks to Amber Kelley for talking to me about
menstruation and bra buying and all things embarrassing.
Thanks to my agent, Barry Goldblatt, for also talking to me about
menstruation and bra buying and all things embarrassing. (Just
kidding! What I mean to say is: thanks to Barry for doing what he
does so very well. ☺) Thanks to sweet Jack for my nightly foot
rubs. And a zillion thanks to Julie Strauss-Gabel, whose editing
insights have only grown richer since becoming a mom.

Most of all, thanks to my crazy family (all generations!)
for giving me such great material to work with.
You guys are nuts. I love you.

Twelve

March

T HE THING ABOUT BIRTHDAYS, especially if you just that very day turned twelve, is that you should make a point of trying to look good. Because twelve is almost thir-teen, and thirteen is a teenager, and teenagers don't strut around with holes in their jeans and ketchup on their shirts.

Well. They did if they were my sister, Sandra, who was fifteen-about-to-turn-sixteen. Her birthday comes next month, which meant that for a delightful three-and-a-half-week period beginning today, she was only three years older than me, instead of four. *Yes!*

Sandra made a show of not caring about her appearance, although it was clear she secretly did. She stayed in the bath-room far longer than any human needed to, and I knew she was in there staring and staring and staring at herself in the mirror: putting on eyeliner and then wiping all but the barest trace of it off; dabbing on the tiniest smidge of Sun Kissed Cheek Stain from the Body Shop; making eyes at her-self and dreaming about Bo, her boyfriend, who told her he liked her just the way she was—natural. So ha ha, the trick was on Bo, but I've learned from Sandra that boys were often like that: clueless, but not necessarily in a bad way. When I am fifteen, I'll probably have a boyfriend, and I'll probably be just like Sandra. I'll want to look pretty, but not like I'm trying.

But today was my birthday, not Sandra's, and I felt like pulling out all the stops. Dressing up usually felt dumb to me—I left that to snooty Gail Grayson and the other sixth-grade go-go girls—but I had a tingly special-day feeling inside. Plus, we were leaving in half an hour for my fancy birthday dinner at Benihana's. Bo was going to meet us there, and so was Dinah, my new best friend. Although it still felt weird calling her that.

I tugged my lemon yellow ballerina skirt from the clippy things on the hanger and wrapped it around my waist. I threaded one tie through the hole at the side, then swooped it around and knotted it in place. When Mom bought this skirt for me six months ago, she had to show me how to make it work, and I'd found it impossibly complicated. Not anymore.

A full-length mirror hung on the inside of my closet door, and I twirled in front of it and watched the fabric swish around my knees. I had scabs from Rollerblading and a scrape from exploring a sewage pipe, but who cared? I could be beautiful *and* tough. I refused to buff away the calluses on my feet, too. Mom said a girl's feet should be soft, but I said, "Uh, no." I was proud of my calluses. I'd worked hard for them. Summer was right around the corner, and I wasn't about to wince my way across the hot concrete when I went to the neighborhood pool. Flip-flops were for wimps. For me, it's barefoot all the way.

I rifled through my clothes until I found my black tank top. Sleek and sophisticated—yeah. People would think I was from New York instead of Atlanta. But when I wiggled into it, I realized something was wrong. It was tight—as in, *really* tight. I flexed my shoulder blades forward and then backward, trying to loosen things up. Then forward and backward again. But what I saw in the mirror was bad. With my herky-jerky shoulders, I looked like a chicken. With breasts.

"Mo-o-om!" I called. "We've got a problem!"

"What?" Mom called back.

"We've got a *problem*!" I yelled.

"Winnie, I can't hear you. If you need me, you're going to have to come here!"

I skittered down the long hall to Mom and Dad's bedroom. My skirt fluttered against my legs.

"Look," I said. Mom was in her bra and underwear, picking out her own outfit, and she was so much curvier than I was. Than I would ever be, I was pretty sure. And that was okay. I didn't want to be curvy. I didn't even want to be . . . bumpy.

Mom turned and took me in. "Winnie, you look *adorable,*" she said. And then, "Oh." And then, "My goodness, Winnie. You're *developing*."

I turned bright red. I could feel it. I crossed my arms high over my chest and said, "What am I supposed to do?"

"Well, you're going to need to pick another top," she said. She put her arm around me and rubbed my bare shoulder. "And I guess we need to go bra shopping, don't we?"

"No no no no no," I said. "Let's not overreact here, all right?" Bras were for go-go girls. Bras were for Gail Grayson, who just last week made a huge stinking deal out of how cool she was because she wore one, while not everyone else in the sixth grade did. Like me and Dinah, to be specific. No way was I going to slink to school with telltale strap lines under my shirt, making Gail believe I actually cared what she thought.

"Sweetie, there's nothing wrong with wearing a bra," Mom said. "It's life. It's the way the world works. It means you're on the brink of womanhood."

"Whoa," I said. I held up my hand, palm out. "Enough, okay?"

She smiled like she thought I was being funny. But I did not want my mother telling me I was on the brink of womanhood. What next? Orthopedic shoes with squishy soles? Dentures?

"You'll probably be getting your period soon, too," Mom said.

"*Beep, beep, beep!* Alert! Alert!" I wiggled out of her grasp and backed toward the door.

"Winnie . . ."

"Got to run. See you!"

I dashed to my room and ducked into my closet, pulling the door shut behind me. I pulled off the tank top, scrunched it into a ball, and dropped it out of sight behind my Little People Castle, which I had yet to pass on to my younger brother, Ty, who was five. I allowed Ty to play with it—together we'd drop Little People through the dungeon's trapdoor and go "*Ahhh!*"—but I wasn't ready to give up possession. Even though Mom said I was too old for it. Even though Sandra said, "Sheesh, Winnie. Grow up already, will you?"

Naked except for my skirt and underwear, I confronted myself in the mirror. It was true: I was no longer flat as a pancake. I had strong arms and a smooth, firm belly and . . .

Boobs.

I was with boob. I was boobful. I was boobed.

I, Winifred Perry, had boobs.

I sank down onto the floor, scrunching my knees up in front of me. How had this happened? I didn't want this. Boobs were for other people, not me. I didn't even like the word *boobs*, although *breasts* was a thousand times worse.

Dinah had boobs, soft little humps that provoked Gail's bra attack on the playground last week. "It's really kind of embarrassing the way certain people bounce around," Gail had said, shooting a sidelong glance at Dinah. "Especially with boys nearby."

Gail's boobs were even bigger than Dinah's. She let her bra straps show on purpose. Sometimes they were purple.

Amanda, who used to be my best friend but who had dumped me for Gail, had also gone the way of the bra, although she did not have boobs.

Which was worse: to have boobs, or not to have boobs?

I didn't want to be boobless *forever*. I just wasn't sure I wanted them now. Today they were starter boobs, no bigger than cotton balls, but what if they kept growing? I thought of a poem Ty had learned at the library, which ended like this: *They grew and they grew and they never stopped, they grew and they grew till the darn things popped!*

The poem was about pea pods. But what if it was in code?

I leaned forward, still looking in the mirror, and bent my arms at the elbow. I placed my bent arms over my chest like big, pendulous breasts. They didn't look like breasts, they looked like elbows, but if I let my sight go hazy, I could create the illusion.

I was ginormous.

The doorknob clicked, and Sandra poked her head into the closet. She saw me on the floor with my elbow-boobs.

"Oh my God. What are you *doing*?" she demanded.

"Nothing!" I scrambled up and grabbed a white button-down.

"It's time to go. Dad's turning the car around."

"I'm getting ready," I said. "A little privacy, please?"

Sandra shook her head. "You just today turned twelve and already you've got attitude? Great, this is just great."

I made a big "ahem" sound.

"Well, hurry," she said. She strode away, leaving the closet door wide open.

At Benihana's, Dinah flittered with excitement. "You look fantastic," she said to me in the waiting area. "You look so *old*. I love your shirt—it looks so cute like that!"

"Thanks," I said. I'd paired a white T-shirt with a white button-down, and I'd tied the ends of the button-down at my waist. My boobs were safely hidden by the double layers, plus the knotted waist of the button-down made the fabric poof out in a way that was very concealing.

"You look nice, too," I told Dinah.

Dinah beamed. She wore a pink dress with a built-in vest. As always, she was one step off in terms of the whole fashion thing. She looked more like she was going to church than going out to dinner. She even carried a small, white leather pocketbook.

"Right this way," the hostess said. She led us to a sunken table at the back of the restaurant. "Shoes here," she said, gesturing to a mat on the floor.

Dinah watched as Dad slipped off his loafers. Mom stepped out of her clogs, and Dinah edged closer to me.

"We have to take our shoes off?" she said.

"Uh-huh," I said. "That's the way they do it in Japan."

"But . . . what if my feet stink?"

"Did you take a shower?" I asked. Dinah's mom died way back when she was a baby, and sometimes she had to be reminded of the basics.

"Yes," she said. "Yesterday I did."

"Then I'm sure your feet are fine," I said. "Anyway, they'll be under the table, not plopped on top with the Poo Poo Platter."

Dinah's eyes widened. "We're having *Poo Poo Platter*?"

"That's Chinese, not Japanese," Sandra said, using her toe to nudge her Chuck Taylors onto the mat. "Stop teasing and be nice."

"She's right," I whispered to Dinah. "We're actually having fish heads."

Sandra rapped me with her knuckles.

"*Ow,*" I said.

The waiter, who had an impressive Fu Manchu mustache, chopped and diced on a steel griddle right in front of us. Oil sizzled, and Dinah shrank back. A snow pea got too hot and exploded; Dinah squealed.

"What's he doing now?" she asked as he slid an upside-down bowl onto the hissing griddle.

"Shrimp," I said. "Yummy yum yum."

The waiter lifted the bowl, and two dozen raw shrimp spilled out, sputtering in the heat. They looked as if they were dancing. I grinned at Dinah, but Dinah didn't grin back.

"Uh . . . Dinah?" I said.

She gulped. "I don't . . . I can't—"

"Do you not like shrimp? Are you allergic?"

"I'm not allergic, I just . . ." Her eyes flew to Bo, who sat on the opposite side of the table with Sandra. He was showing Ty how to bounce water up inside a straw by tapping the end with his finger.

I lowered my voice. "You just what?"

Dinah gave me a pleading look. "I'm scared of them."

A whoop burst out of me. "Of *shrimp*? You're scared of shrimp?"

"Shhh," she said. "They're so pale. And they've got . . . veins."

"Really *big* veins," I said. "Help! They're coming to get me! Attack of the veins!"

She giggled despite herself. "Don't let him give me any, okay? I mean it."

In part she was being goofy, but in part she meant it, too. She was funny that way, always wanting me to protect her—which usually I didn't mind because it made me feel important. It was something I noticed, though. My friendship with Dinah was so different from my friendship with Amanda, who'd been much more of an . . . equal.

Ooo, shove that thought back down. Dinah was an equal, too. Just a different kind of equal.

Dad clinked his fork against his glass, and I was glad for the distraction. I sat up tall and nudged Dinah to do the same.

"A toast," Dad said.

"Hear, hear!" said Ty. He loved making toasts.

"To my wonderful daughter on her twelfth birthday," Dad said.

"Oh God, here we go," said Sandra.

"May she learn the value of a tidy room and a tidy desk, and may she realize that when it comes to stuffing the toilet with gummy worms, her father does indeed know best."

"Da-a-ad," I said. I'd put gummy worms in the toilet *once*, when I was like Ty's age.

"May she always stay true to her kind and generous heart," he said. "And may she stay our little girl forever."

He gazed at me. There was love in his eyes, and it made me embarrassed, but happy, too.

"Cheers!" cried Ty, lifting his Shirley Temple. "Everybody clink!"

I clinked my glass with Dinah's, and then with Dad's. Then Mom's and Sandra's and Bo's and Ty's.

"Happy birthday, sweetie," Mom said.

"Yeah, yeah, happy birthday," said Sandra.

"Happy birthday," said the Fu Manchu waiter. He flipped a sizzling pink shrimp at me, but it missed my plate and landed on Dinah's. Or maybe that's what he intended all along. Dinah shrieked, and everyone laughed.

Ty went to bed at nine, and at ten, Mom and Dad retired to their room to watch the news. By eleven, I was pretty tired, and I think Dinah was, too, but we weren't the slightest bit ready to go to sleep. Punch-drunk, Mom would have called us. Everything I said made Dinah laugh, and everything Dinah said made me laugh. Sandra kept stomping into my room to tell us to be quiet, and each time she looked grumpier and grumpier. The last time she had a mud mask smeared over her face, and I said, "Better wipe that frown off, young lady, or it'll stick like that." Dinah about busted a gut.

After Sandra left, I said, "She puts that on to clean her pores. Isn't that weird, to use mud to clean your face?"

"She's so pretty," Dinah said. She scratched my cat, Sweetie-Pie, behind the ears, and Sweetie-Pie head-butted her in pleasure. "Is it fun having a sister who's so pretty?"

"*Ehh*," I said. Sandra *was* pretty, but mainly she was just Sandra. "Want me to see if she'll let us use some of her mask?"

"Yeah!" Dinah said.

"It's really neat," I said, getting to my feet. "It tightens on your face until you can't smile, and it feels like you're paralyzed. Hold on, I'll be right back."

I padded across the hall to Sandra's room, but she was on the phone with Bo. I held up my finger to mean, "Just one little thing? Real quick?" She scowled and turned her back to me.

Well, I thought to myself. *How rude.* I walked in plain sight to her bathroom and grabbed the tub of mask, then darted in pouncy, tiptoe steps back across the hall.

"Mission accomplished!" I announced. I plopped down on the floor, and Dinah scooted closer.

"So what do we do?" she asked.

I picked up Sweetie-Pie and tossed her onto the bed, because mud and fur don't mix. Then I unscrewed the lid of the container. "We smear it all over, and then we let it dry." I wiped a fingerful across my cheek. It was cool and oozy. "Now that I'm twelve, I guess I better start thinking about these things. Pores and stuff."

"How does it feel being twelve?" Dinah asked. "Does it feel different?"

I liked the way she was regarding me, as if I were the wise one because I was older.

"Hmm," I said. "Mainly it feels the same . . . but yeah, I guess it is different." I hesitated, then said, "My mom says it's time for me to get a bra."

"Really?"

I shrugged inside my oversized Braves nightshirt. "Not like tomorrow or anything. I mean, it's not *desperate*."

Dinah swiped on one last blob of mud, and a little got in her hair. "Whoops," she said.

"In fact I'm kind of hoping she'll forget about it," I said. "Because once you start wearing a bra, you can't turn back. It's like shaving your legs."

"It is?"

"Well, with legs, the hair comes back pricklier once you start shaving, so you really shouldn't start unless you're ready to commit forever and ever. Same with bras."

"Your boobs come back pricklier?" Dinah said.

I giggled. "Uh-huh. Like cactuses."

She giggled, too. "What are you *talking* about?"

"Imagine if a boy tried to touch them. '*Ooo*, baby, I'm feeling so romantic—*ouch*!'"

"Stop making me laugh!" she said. "You're making my face crack!"

"You look like the Creature from the Black Lagoon. Want to see?" I scrambled up and grabbed my hand mirror from my bureau. I very sneakily grabbed something else, too: a little souvenir from Benihana's that I'd plucked from my plate and wrapped in a paper napkin to bring home. I hadn't known what I'd do with it until now.

"Close your eyes," I said, "and don't open them till I say 'three.' Okay? One, two . . . three!"

Dinah opened her eyes. She saw the shrimp dangling in front of her nose.

"*Eeeee!*" she screamed.

I wiggled it closer. "It's coming to get you! It's coming to get you!"

"Nooo!"

Sweetie-Pie meowed in alarm.

Sandra burst into the room. "God!" she complained. "For the fifty millionth time, do you have to be so—" She stopped, noticing our cakey faces. "Did you use my mud mask? Without asking?"

I widened my eyes. In my sweetest, nicest voice, I said, "Er . . . care for a shrimp?"

Sandra took in the limp pink shrimp swaying between my fingers. Disgust layered itself over her outrage. "You are *so* immature," she said.

"*Au contraire, mon frère,*" I protested. "In case you've forgotten, I am twelve years old. I'm on the brink of womanhood."

"Could have fooled me," she retorted. She snatched the container of mask, stormed out of the room, and slammed the door.

"Sandra, Sandra, Sandra," I said, shaking my head. "Do you have to be so loud?"

Dinah collapsed in hysterics.

April

"NOW THAT I'M TWELVE, can you take me to get my ears pierced?" I asked Mom.

"What?" she said. Ty whacked her with his plastic sword, and she attempted to fend him off. A piece of green pepper fell from the kitchen counter.

"Your arm is your sword," he told her, "and your stomach is your shield. It's time to face your fears!"

"When are you going to take me to get my license?" Sandra demanded, breaking in to get Mom's attention. "You promised we'd go yesterday."

I yanked on Mom's sleeve. "You said when I was twelve, and I've been twelve for over three weeks!"

"And I've been sixteen for two entire days," Sandra said. "Every single person in the world gets to get their driver's license on their exact birthday. Everyone but me!"

"Your birthday was on a Sunday," I pointed out.

"And today is *Tuesday*," Sandra said. "As in two full days later." She turned to Mom. "Can we *please* go get my license?"

"I asked first!" I said. "I've been waiting even longer!"

"Ka-pow!" Ty said, smacking Mom below the knee. "Your leg is gone! You have to fall down!"

"*Enough!*" Mom cried.

We fell silent. Ty hesitated, then poked Mom with the tip of the sword. Mom snatched it and plunked it on the counter.

"Good heavens," Mom said. "You children are driving me crazy."

Sandra huffed indignantly, and I shared her pain. We were hardly "children."

Mom closed her eyes. She inhaled. She was doing her relaxation breath, which we were all familiar with. She exhaled calmly and slowly. She opened her eyes.

"Now," she said. "Ty, no sword fighting in the house." She turned to me. "And, Winnie, are you *sure* you want to get your ears pierced? Are you absolutely positive?"

"Mo-o-om," I said. She couldn't get it through her head that yes, I was sure, and that nothing she could say would change my mind. Not that she hadn't given it her best shot. Over the weekend she'd modeled a fake ear out of Ty's Silly Putty to give me a visual demonstration of what I was in for.

"This is your ear," she'd said. And it did look remarkably like an ear—even the color was appropriately skin-toned. She used her fingernail to carve out a too-big hole in the lobe, then said, "And this is what will happen if you wear earrings. Your ear will stretch, like this." She pulled on the lobe, and it stretched like taffy. It became a tribal woman's ear in *National Geographic*. Then the Silly Putty reached its snapping point, and the whole lobe popped off, leaving a mutilated half ear with an unnaturally smooth scar.

"You see?" Mom had said.

Now I took Mom's knife and placed it by the green peppers. I put my hands on her shoulders. "Repeat after me," I said. "Ear piercing will not lead to disfigurement. Ear piercing is normal and good."

"Hello?" Sandra said impatiently. "My driver's license?"

Mom sighed. She got a Ziploc bag from the drawer and scraped the peppers into it. She sealed it and put it in the fridge. Then she faced the three of us and said, "Here's what we'll do. We'll go to the mall and get Winnie's ears pierced, and Sandra, you can drive. And afterward we'll stop by the Department of Motor Vehicles. Everybody satisfied?"

"Can I bring my sword?" Ty asked.

"You can bring it in the car, but not into the mall," Mom declared.

"Deal," Ty said.

On the way to Lenox Square, I gave Sandra helpful hints about her driving.

"Green light means go," I said when Sandra was slow to start up at a traffic light. I said it very pleasantly, but Sandra scowled nonetheless.

"Oops, don't hit the pedestrian!" I exclaimed as we passed a man walking his dog.

"He's fifteen feet away!" Sandra protested. "He's on the sidewalk!"

"Crazy driver!" Ty said.

"Winnie and Ty, stop distracting your sister," Mom scolded. "Driving is very serious business. One wrong turn and you could ruin a life forever."

"We know, we know, we know," I said. Earlobes popping off, innocent bystanders getting killed in the blink of an eye—in Mom Land there was disaster lurking around every corner.

"My cousin Laetitia was killed when she was two years old," Mom said. "Her own father backed over her in his pickup truck." She twisted around to eye me from the front seat. "Do you think a day goes by when he doesn't wish he could go back in time?"

I'd heard many times about Laetitia, so I didn't bother to respond. I felt extremely sad about Laetitia, and morbidly fascinated as well. Did she cry out? Was it quick? Did her father feel a horrible bump and know immediately that his world had changed?

"Imagine how horrible you would feel if you took a life," Mom went on. "Or if you maimed someone. Imagine how horrible you would feel if you caused an accident and a ten-year-old boy fell into a coma and never came out. It happens every day!"

"What ten-year-old boy?" Ty asked.

"Okay, Mom, we get the point," Sandra said. I noticed with interest that she was gripping the steering wheel more tightly than usual.

"*What* ten-year-old boy?" Ty asked again. "Tell that story!"

"Could everybody please stop talking?" Sandra said. "Or I'm going to have a wreck for real!"

"Sandra, if you think you're going to have a wreck, then pull over," Mom said. "You should never drive when you're incapacitated. Just last week a man had a heart attack in his car and killed four teenagers."

"Mom!" Sandra complained.

Mom settled into her seat with the air of someone who has spoken the truth, and too bad if it was painful. "You need to be careful, that's all I'm saying."

On the escalator that led to the second floor of the mall, Mom glanced at her watch and said, "You know, Winnie, while we're here we could take care of some other shopping. It really is time we got you a—"

"La la la la la," I said to drown her out. "Look! Isn't that a cute bunny, Ty? Isn't that a cute bunny?"

"Time she got a what?" Sandra asked.

Ty regarded me with disdain. "I'm not a baby," he said, "so you don't have to talk to me like that. And there isn't any bunny."

"In the toy store," I said to Ty. And to Sandra, "*Nothing.*" I glared at Mom.

Mom widened her eyes, like *I'm sorry, I didn't know*. But she should have. Nobody wants to go bra shopping with her scoffing older sister.

At Claire's Boutique, the saleslady set me loose in the rows and rows of sparkling earrings. She said not to pick danglies, but that I should be sure to get fourteen-karat-gold posts for my very first pair. She recommended delicate gold balls.

"Too boring," I said.

"Too WASPy," Sandra said.

"Huh?" I said.

"WASPy," Sandra said. "As in a White Anglo Saxon Protestant?"

I still didn't get it.

"Hoity-toity rich-girl stuff, like going to the country club and having a tennis date with Muffy. '*Oh, dahling, you look so adorable in your precious gold earrings.*'"

"Sandra," Mom said.

"I like these," I said, selecting a pair of tiny gold flowers with pale blue stones in the middle. "Will they work?"

"They'll do just fine," the saleslady said. I wondered if she was WASPy, and decided she was. She had a big bust and sensible shoes. Her own earrings were prim gold bows.

She used a pen to dot both my ears, then gave me a mirror so that I could check the placement.

"Looks good," I said. Jitters started up in my stomach.

She loaded the gun with earring number one, and *pop*! In it went, just like that. There was a pinching sensation, but it honestly didn't hurt at all.

"Can I do the other one?" Ty asked.

"*No!*" the saleslady and I said at the same time. She repeated the procedure for earring number two, and then she handed me the mirror once again.

"There you go," she said. "What do you think?"

I turned my head from side to side. Glints of light danced off the earrings.

"Great," I said.

"What does she need to do about upkeep?" Mom asked. "That is part of our agreement, that she'll be responsible for taking care of them. Should she swab them with hydrogen peroxide?"

The saleslady shook her head as she rang up our total. "That's no longer recommended. She needs to twist them every night before bed for a week, but only use hydrogen peroxide if they get infected."

"If they get infected, your earlobes will fall off," Sandra said.

Mom nodded. "True," she said.

The saleslady opened her mouth, then shut it.

"Ha ha," I said. I looked completely and utterly fabulous, and I knew it. I felt on top of the world.

Our next stop was the DMV, but when we got there, Sandra chickened out.

"It's too late," she said, not getting out of the driver's seat. "They're going to close any minute."

"It's a quarter till four," Mom said. "They don't close until five."

"There could be a long line," Sandra said. She swallowed and wouldn't look at any of us.

"Sandra, what's going on?" Mom asked.

Sandra didn't answer. Her spine was stiff, and I realized with surprise that she was scared. My sister, Sandra, was scared.

"It's because of all that stuff you said," I told Mom. "About how she could kill someone with one false move."

"That's not it," Sandra said angrily.

"Oh, Sandra," Mom said. "I didn't mean to worry you, sweetie."

Sandra made a noise of disbelief, which I happened to agree with. Mom loved to worry us. She had a horror story for every occasion.

"Anyway, I was scared about getting my ears pierced, but I did it just the same," I said.

"Yeah," Ty said. "And I was scared when you talked about wasps, but I was brave just like Winnie."

I looked at him in confusion. What was he talking about? Then I got it: *WASPs,* as in White Anglo Saxon Protestants. I giggled.

"Not that kind of wasps, you doof," Sandra said. "And

anyway, you were not scared. You were just jealous of the saleslady's gun."

"Guns are a bad idea," Ty said piously. "You should only use guns if you're a bad guy."

"Oh, good Lord," Sandra said, putting her head in her hands.

"Sandra, if you're going to take your driver's test, you need to go in and do it now," Mom said. "Otherwise we need to go home."

"Fine, we'll go home," Sandra said. She turned the key in the ignition.

Mom was surprised. "Are you sure?"

Sandra put the car in reverse and pulled out of the parking spot. "I'll do it soon," she said. "Just not today."

"Did you get your license?" I asked Sandra the next day when I got home from school.

Sandra gave me her "you're an idiot" look. "When would I have gotten it? I've been at school all day just like you."

"Oh," I said. "Well, are you going to?"

"I'm too tired. We had to run three miles in PE."

"You're too worn out to drive a car?"

"Leave me alone," she said.

The next day she hung out with Bo and conveniently forgot to come home until 5:30, after the DMV had closed. And on Thursday, she had an earth-science assignment to complete concerning the Ring of Fire. The Ring of Fire, she informed me, was a big circle in the Pacific Ocean where there was a lot of volcanic activity. California was part of the Ring of Fire. That was why there were so many earthquakes there.

"Uh-huh," I said. "And this has to do with your driver's license because . . . ?"

"Eighty-one percent of the world's earthquakes happen in the Ring of Fire!" she exclaimed. "We're talking major world disasters! Do you really think this is an appropriate time to be discussing the DMV?"

While she slaved away on her project—or more likely IM'd with her friends and chowed down on Oreos—I went out into the beautiful spring day for a bike ride. It was crazy that Sandra was being such a wimp, I thought as I cruised down Woodward Way. Usually she was so tough. Usually she was the one who could do anything.

I turned right on Peachtree Battle and stood to pedal up the hill. My muscles burned in a way that made me feel strong. Down the steep slope to Sagamore Drive, the wind whipping my hair. I'd worn a helmet out the back door for Mom's sake, but I'd stashed it in the bushes when I got to the bottom of the driveway. I couldn't stand having a helmet on. I felt so much freer without.

As I biked around Memorial Park, I reached up to check the posts of my earrings, to make sure they were still there. Today during lunch, Gail Grayson's hand had flown to her ear and she'd cried out in alarm. One of her earrings had fallen out and was nowhere to be found.

"My *diamond*," she had wailed when everyone gathered around. She held out the other one, which she'd removed for safekeeping, but folded her fingers over it when Dinah got too close. "My dad gave them to me. They came from South Africa. They cost two thousand dollars!"

My homeroom teacher, Mr. Hutchinson, shared a glance with Ms. Russell.

"Why in the world did you wear a two-thousand-dollar pair of earrings to school?" Ms. Russell asked.

"Yeah," I said.

"Be*cause*," Gail said. She glared at me in a way that reminded me we weren't friends and never would be. "I happen to think high fashion goes a little further than Claire's Boutique, that's why."

"Ouch," said Louise. She loved seeing other people get taken down.

Then, from under the table, Amanda had called, "I found it, I found it!" She backed out on her hands and knees and held up the glittering stone.

"Amanda, *thank* you!" Gail said. "Omigod, thank you so so so much!" She flung herself on Amanda in a stumble-back hug.

"I thought you said you looked there already," I said.

"I did," Gail said.

"It was smushed into a bread crumb," Amanda said. "Someone must have stepped on it."

"Someone clumsy and stupid," Gail said.

I'd pressed my lips together, not proud of what I was feeling. I wished Gail's earring hadn't been found. I wished she'd been taught a lesson—that it hurts when you lose something special.

I pumped hard on my bicycle, not wanting to think about that anymore. Losing a friend, the way I'd lost Amanda, was a lot worse than losing an earring. It wasn't as bad as losing someone to a car accident, but it still made my heart ache. Especially when something happened like that hug.

Mom should have warned us about that. She should have warned us that *everything* was dangerous unless you shut yourself up in your house and never came out.

Actually, at some point or another, she probably had.

I leaned sideways as the road curved, and a squirrel scampered in front of me. I reacted on instinct, jerking the handlebars right and then left to avoid it. I didn't have time to think.

And then, *squish*. My tire bumped over it. Its soft little belly. It was plump, like a grape, and then it wasn't. There was a texture to the squish that made my throat close.

I squeezed the hand brakes and squealed to a stop. Straddling the bike, I turned around. The squirrel lay motionless, fat and furry except in the spot I'd run over it. Oh God.

The squirrel's paw twitched, and a weird cold sweat popped out in my armpits. What was I supposed to do for a half-smushed squirrel that was still alive?

My heart thudded.

I hadn't meant to hurt it.

My hands were clenching and unclenching my brakes, and I didn't even realize it until the metal dug deep into my palms.

The squirrel flicked its tail, then scrambled to its feet and darted into the tall grass on the side of the street. I blinked. Where the squirrel had been, there was nothing: no blood, no guts, no tufts of fur.

A wave of repulsion washed over me.

"You okay?" a runner asked as he jogged by.

"Uh-huh," I said. My body felt boneless, and I got off my bike and sat down.

After several minutes, I heaved myself up. I grasped my bike by the handlebars and trudged with it all the way home.

The next day, I went to Dinah's after school. I told her about the squirrel, and she didn't laugh or say "ew."

"That's so amazing that it came back to life," she said.

"I know," I said.

"I mean, it's like . . . a miracle," she said.

I nodded. "I know."

She regarded me with something close to awe. Then she

remembered the Ritz cracker in her hand and squirted on a dollop of Cheez Whiz. She offered it to me.

"Thanks," I said.

"When something like that happens, you have to take it as a sign," Dinah said seriously.

"Of what?" I asked. I liked this about Dinah, that I could talk to her about real things without any elaborate eye rolling. She wasn't afraid to speak truly. Sometimes it got her in trouble, like during PE when she asked what a "douche" was, and, when pressed, didn't take it back and pretend she'd been joking. "I really don't know," she'd said to Chantelle, who'd brought it up in the first place. "Just tell me!"

Dinah put down the Cheez Whiz. She looked at me, and I stopped chewing. It got quiet. I had the sense she was going to say something important.

"I don't know," she said at last. "But *something*. And you probably won't even know it until it happens."

The Ritz cracker was mealy in my mouth. I swallowed, then used my tongue to work out what was left.

"Want another?" she asked.

When Dinah's dad dropped me off at the end of the afternoon, I was alert for changes big or small. I didn't know if I believed in Dinah's sign business, but it was fun to think about. Maybe Mom had bought me a treat, a new shirt from the mall or my favorite flavor of fruit leather. She did that sometimes to say yahoo for a good week of school.

But Mom was fixing dinner like normal—homemade chicken pot pie with bonus crust. Ty was applying sparkly heart stickers up and down his arm, and Sandra was sitting at the table doing her homework. She lifted her head when I plunked down my backpack. She followed me with her eyes as I got myself a glass of orange juice.

"What?" I said. I pulled out a chair and joined her at the table. "Is my hair sticking up funny?"

"Aren't you going to ask if I got my license?" she said.

"Oh my gosh," I said. "Did you?"

"Yes," she said accusingly.

"That's great! Congratulations!"

"Yeah, whatever."

I frowned. If she got her license, why was she acting so sour?

"Show her," Mom said to Sandra, barely suppressing her smile.

Sandra flipped the piece of laminated plastic my way. It was smooth and authentic, and I was impressed. The picture wasn't great—she looked a little bug-eyed—but it wasn't terrible.

"Read what it says under 'weight,'" Mom said.

I scanned the card. EYES: BLUE. HAIR: BLOND. WEIGHT: 1000.

A laugh blurbled out of me before I could help it. Mom laughed, too.

Sandra scowled. "It's supposed to say one *hundred*. The stupid lady typed in an extra zero."

Delighted, I imagined Sandra at the tremendous weight of a thousand pounds. She'd be a giant blueberry. She could go and join the circus.

"I'm going to get a new one," Sandra said. "I'll say this one got lost, and I'll just pay to do it all over again."

"Sandra, *no*," I said. I clutched the license to my heart. "It's so much better this way!"

"Oh yeah? How do you figure that?"

"Because it's so funny. It's one of a kind." I had a brainstorm. "In fact, it's a sign!"

"A *sign*? Of what?"

"Of the fact that you're going to be a very good driver, because the bad thing has already happened and it was *this*." I tapped the license. "So that means no accidents or maiming or loss of life. Isn't that good?"

"*If* you're careful," Mom interjected. She wagged her flour-covered spoon.

"Mo-o-om," Sandra groaned.

"Sometimes bad things happen even when you *are* careful," she went on. "I'm sorry, but they do."

"But sometimes they don't," I said. "Sometimes they get up and walk away and everything's just fine!"

"Exsqueeze me?" Sandra said.

I held her license out of reach. "I am very proud of you for facing your fears and taking your driver's test, just like I am very proud of me for getting my ears pierced."

"Are you proud of me?" Ty asked, glancing up from his sparkly hearts.

"Yes," I pronounced. "I am proud of you for lining your stickers up so neatly and symmetrically." I cleared my throat. "Now. Sandra. If I give you this back, do you promise not to get a new one?"

"Give it to me," she said.

"*Do* you?"

She nabbed it from my fingers and smiled victoriously.

"Maybe I will and maybe I won't," she said. "You'll just have to wait and see."

May

ON A THURSDAY EVENING near the end of May, Mom did the unthinkable. She announced, smack in the middle of dinner, that it was time to take me bra shopping.

"Mom!" I protested.

"Nope, no arguing," Mom said, pointing at me with an asparagus spear. "You're a growing girl. Your graduation ceremony is in two weeks. We're getting you a bra tomorrow."

My cheeks could have lit a fire, that's how hot they were. A Girl Scout could have roasted marshmallows on them. And it wasn't just the fact of a bra, which was terrible enough on its own. It was that she was saying all this in front of Dad and Sandra and Ty, who now gazed at me with varying levels of interest.

"A bra," Dad said jovially. "That's terrific. Get me one, too, will you?"

Ty's eyes widened as he absorbed this new idea, that maybe men *did* wear bras. "I want one, I want one!" he said.

Mom frowned at Dad. "Bras are not for little boys," she said. "*Or* grown men."

"I can't believe you don't have one already," Sandra said. She munched on her chicken tender, which Mom bought at Whole Foods and then pretended were made from scratch. "You're such a throwback."

"What's a throwback?" asked Ty.

"Someone who doesn't get a bra until sixth grade," Sandra said. "Kind of like an ape."

"Sandra," Mom scolded.

I focused on my corn, which looked like teeth. Yellow kernels, then pale up at the top with a flimsy rim of skin. Like they'd been pulled from someone's mouth and plopped in a pile on my plate.

"Winnie?" Mom said, at long last realizing that I wasn't joining in on the hilarity. "Are you okay?"

I didn't answer. I was too angry. Didn't she know that my "growing body" should not be discussed at the dinner table?

"You don't want to look different from everybody else," she went on, softening her voice in a way that made things ten thousand times worse. "I know it's hard, and it's not necessarily something that's good about the world. But, sweetie, it's easier if you fit in."

"Fine," I said. My lips hardly moved.

"What, honey?"

I raised my eyes and sent her a look that I hoped would scorch right through her retinas. "I said *fine*."

She held my gaze. It was a battle of wills—at least that's

how it felt to me—until she curved her mouth downward to show her disappointment.

I don't care, I said to myself. *Don't care, don't care, don't care.*

"There's a girl in my class I do not like," Ty announced. He squirted a blob of ketchup onto his plate. "She's new. She moved here from Texas the day after this day."

"You mean the day *before* today," Sandra said. Ty was always messing up his yesterdays and tomorrows.

"She has a bad smile," Ty said. "Like this." He pushed his lower teeth out past his upper teeth and grimaced, squinching up his eyes. Dad cough-laughed, and a splatter of mashed potatoes hit my arm. I wiped myself off in silence. I was mad at him, too.

"Does she smile like that on purpose?" Sandra asked.

"Yes," Ty said. "She does it all the time. Her name is Taffy."

"*Taffy?*" Sandra said. "Ugh, that's unfortunate."

Mom stood up. "Does anyone want any more chicken, or are you ready for dessert?"

"Dessert," Sandra and Ty said together.

"Winnie?" Mom said. There was too much patience in her voice.

"I'm full."

She waited. "Then you can ask to be excused."

"May I please be excused?"

She sighed. "You may."

Later, after a rerun of *7th Heaven* that I didn't really watch, I went to Ty's room to talk about Taffy. It *was* an unfortunate name, but I felt wounded on her behalf. Maybe she couldn't help the way she smiled—had anyone considered that? Anyway, was looking different really such a crime?

"Hi," I said, flopping down on the floor beside him.

"I'm having bonus playtime because I got my pj's on before the timer went off," he said. "And brushed teeth. *And* put my clothes in the dirty-clothes basket."

"Good job," I said.

"Want to play with me?" He held out a gray plastic knight. "You can be this guy. He can step on hot lava and not even melt."

I accepted the knight. I made him walk a little, but with no sound effects. "Listen, about Taffy," I said.

Ty came at me with his own knight, which was red. "*Brrrng!*" he cried. "*Wa-choo!*"

"She probably has an underbite. She probably can't help the way she smiles."

"She says no one will play with her on the playground, but I don't want to either," Ty said. He karate-chopped my knight. "Take that! Whack, whack!"

"When I was in kindergarten, there was a kid in my class named Jared who had really greasy hair," I said. "Everybody was mean to him. It made him cry."

"That's not nice," Ty said.

"He ended up moving to California, which is too bad, because that's where all the earthquakes are."

"Oh," Ty said.

"It's in the Ring of Fire."

"That boy's hair?"

"No, California. Because of all the underwater volcano explosions."

"He could die," Ty said. "Right, Winnie?"

"That's right," I said. "And there was another boy, his name was Charlie, who had an actual steel plate in his head. He could bang on it like this"—I rapped my skull—"and it made a hollow sound. The kids were *super* mean to him."

I had Ty's attention. There hadn't really been a boy named Charlie in my kindergarten class (well, there was, but he didn't have a steel plate in his head), but I thought it served my point.

"Did he move to California, too?" Ty asked.

"Not that I know of."

"What *did* he do?"

"I don't know. He probably grew up to be very sad."

"He might have turned into a criminal," Ty suggested.

"He might have," I said. "That's why you need to be nice to Taffy. You don't want her to grow up to be a criminal, do you?"

"No."

"People can't help being different. There's nothing *wrong* with being different."

"I know."

"Okay, then." I tossed him the gray knight, then stretched over and gave him a kiss.

Ty swiped at his cheek, and I said, "Ty!"

"I only wiped the slobber off," Ty insisted. "Not the kiss."

"Yeah, right," I said.

He smiled his sweet-boy smile. "Night, Winnie. Love you."

"Love you, too," I said.

Dinah adored the mall. Amanda, before we stopped being best friends, seriously adored the mall. I, on the other hand, did not. I pretended to sometimes, because I didn't want to be a wet blanket. And there were some mall things that were admittedly cool: the fountain, the pet store, Chick-fil-A.

But plain old shopping? Boring with a capital B, especially if you were with your mother, and especially if she insisted on checking out the boring women's fashions at boring Neiman Marcus with its boring racks of boring old-lady boringness.

But boring was better than another B-word, which I hoped Mom would somehow forget, and which of course she did not, despite the gift with purchase at the Clinique counter.

"All right, Winnie, time to focus on you," she said as I trailed her into Macy's junior department.

"I'm tired," I said. "I need to sit down."

"You can sit down in the dressing room," Mom replied. "Now let's see, I suppose they have a lingerie section for pre-teens. Do they call it 'lingerie' at that age?"

I pretended I wasn't with her. Did she have to be so loud?

"Excuse me, miss?" Mom said to the nearest salesclerk. "We're looking for a bra for a twelve-year-old. Can you point us in the right direction?"

"*Mom,*" I said through gritted teeth.

"What?" Mom said.

"You don't have to *say* it," I said.

She closed her eyes as if she were aggrieved. She'd done that a lot this particular excursion.

The salesclerk glanced from Mom to me. She was young, which made it worse. Her clothes were very hip.

"No worries, we have a great selection right over here," she said. She led us past the prom dresses to a section full of socks, then past the socks to a section where everything was shiny or lacy or flowered. She pulled free a pink bra with a bow at the center. It had no cups, just flat pink triangles. "Isn't this adorable?"

"No," I said.

"Winnie," Mom warned, shooting me a look.

The salesclerk laughed. "That's okay. I remember how embarrassing it was getting my first bra." She smiled at me as if she were my pal, which she wasn't. She selected another bra. "How about this one? I love the little Care Bears."

Care Bears? On a bra? She had to be joking. But no, there they were, marching across the elastic band with their lollipops and rainbows. How old did she think I was—two?

"No," I said.

"This one?" Red lace this time. And padded.

I looked to Mom for help, then immediately looked away, remembering that she was the enemy. But that left me feeling awfully alone, and stupid, and now in the most annoying of ways I felt as if I might cry. I wrapped my arms around my chest and gazed at the prom dresses.

"We'll take a look, and we'll holler if we need you," Mom said. *Holler.* She actually said *holler.*

"You got it," said the salesclerk.

Mom waited until she was gone. Then she said, "Winnie, stop being such a pill. I'm sorry you don't want to be here, but you might as well make the best of it. Now. Do you see any styles you like?"

"No," I said. I couldn't help it—it was the truth.

She pushed her hand through her hair. "What exactly is the problem? Can you explain to me *why* you're so against getting a bra?"

Because they're wrong, I wanted to say. *Because they've got straps that show through, and people will see. Because Gail wears a bra, and Amanda even though she doesn't need one, and I don't want to be someone like that. Because tomboys are much cooler, and I want to be a tomboy, and anyway, why* don't *boys have to wear bras? Or something equally horrible, at any rate. And jockstraps don't count, whatever they are.*

I don't want a bra because I don't want anyone looking at that part of my body, or thinking about that part of my body, or acknowledging that part of my body, even my mother. Because yes, I want to be a woman someday, but not now. Because I don't want to have to worry about any of it. Because it just isn't fair.

There were lots of reasons I didn't want a bra, even if I didn't know many of them until that minute. And even if I wasn't about to say any of them out loud.

So I shrugged. Mom got even more exasperated.

"Winnie, this is getting old," she said.

"Then let's go home," I said. I strode out of the "girls' intimates" section and ran smack into the last person in the world I would have chosen to see at that terrible moment: Gail Grayson, examining a blue sequined prom dress.

"Gail," I said without meaning to.

"Winnie," she said. First she looked surprised, and then displeased, because that's how she always looked when it came to me. Like she smelled something sour.

My brain went into overdrive. How long had she been here? What had she heard?

"If you get that one, you'll have to get a strapless," Gail's mom said, appearing by the rack. She had platinum hair and gold hoop earrings. "Although possibly your black bra from

Paris Houghton might work. Isn't it the one with removable straps?"

"Mom, this is Winnie," Gail said with zero enthusiasm. "Winnie, this is my mom."

"Hi," I said.

"I'm Ellen," Mom said, joining us and stepping forward to shake Mrs. Grayson's hand.

"So nice to meet you," Mrs. Grayson said. "I'm Noreen." She smiled a wide wrecking-ball smile, ready to knock down anything in its path. She must have been to a tanning salon, because she was midsummer bronzed and it was still the middle of spring.

"Gail's going to her cousin's Sweet Sixteen," Mrs. Grayson said. "The theme is Las Vegas."

"Mom, they don't care," Gail said.

"Forty thousand dollars," Mrs. Grayson confided. "That's what Kiki's daddy is paying for this shindig. Can you believe it?"

"That's more than my wedding," Mom said.

Mrs. Grayson bark-laughed. "I know! It's crazy!"

Gail's cheeks colored, unless I imagined it.

"So what are you two wild women shopping for?" Mrs. Grayson asked, referring, apparently, to me and Mom.

"Oh," Mom said. "Well . . ."

Don't, I begged her silently. I got that pre-diarrhea feeling of desperation, because Gail would be the worst person in the universe—the *worst*—to know I was bra shopping.

"I dragged Winnie to check out the spring shoe sale, actually," Mom said. "We figured we'd check out the junior department while we were here."

"How *fun*," Mrs. Grayson said. "Don't you just love shopping with your daughter? Don't you wish you could fit in these darling fashions?"

Gail looked behind me at the intimates section, then back at me, her expression craftily innocent. "I thought you were shopping for a bra," she said.

"We figured we'd take a peek," Mom said smoothly.

"I thought you didn't believe in bras," Gail went on. She was referring to a remark I'd made on the playground once, the time she was mean to Dinah.

"Don't believe in *bras*?" Mrs. Grayson said. She blinked her overmascaraed eyes. "Now listen. You girls think you'll stay young and firm forever, but you won't. You have to wear a bra, or you'll sag."

"I don't think Winnie has to worry about that yet," Gail said.

"Oh yes she does," Mrs. Grayson said. She zeroed in on me. "You most certainly do, Wendy. It's never too early to start caring about your appearance."

"It's Winnie," I said.

"What's that?"

"It's Winnie. Not Wendy."

Gail smirked. I got the sense she thought her mom and I were stupid, both. I was filled with a dislike for her that swirled and mixed with my embarrassment.

Mom's hand tightened on the handle of her Neiman Marcus bag. "Well, we've got to get going. Winnie? You ready?"

We walked right out of Macy's, and then we continued through the mall and into the parking lot, where I climbed mutely into the car with Mom. The air conditioner kicked on at full blast when she turned on the engine. Neither of us mentioned the fact that we were leaving without what we'd come for.

"I didn't like that girl," Mom said after merging into the afternoon traffic. "She's pretty on the outside, but I have a feeling she isn't very pretty on the inside." She glanced at me. "Am I right?"

"Uh-huh," I said.

"She's not going to have any friends if that's the way she acts."

"She only acts that way to certain people," I said. "She has lots of friends."

"*Hmmph,*" Mom said. She flicked her blinker and scooted into the far right lane. "That makes me like her even less."

In the end, I got three bras—one white, one black, one tan— at Target. The tan one was gross and I didn't want it, but Mom said that was the only color that wouldn't show under white clothes. She called it "nude," not tan. I thought to myself how much there was to learn about being a woman, most of it kind of silly.

Mom seemed more relaxed at Target than at Macy's, commenting that Target had "surprisingly good" lingerie. I felt more relaxed, too. I felt safe there with its bright wide aisles and displays of random items, like Sno-Kone machines. Mom let me get one as an impulse buy, along with a set of four fancy plastic cups with matching spoons and a three-pack of flavored syrups.

"It'll be perfect for summer," I said, eager to get home and try it out.

"Will you share with Ty?" Mom asked, acting motherish and in-control-of-the-purse-strings even though the Sno-Kone box was already in the cart.

"Yes," I said. "And Sandra. I'll be the one to make them, but I'll let them pick which flavor." The box almost, but not entirely, obscured the limp collection of bras, but I wasn't so worried about them anymore, even though anyone looking would have known exactly what they were. I don't know why—they just no longer seemed so important.

That evening, over strawberry-kiwi Sno-Kones, I told Ty about the special escalator at Target that was just for shopping carts.

"The people go up one escalator, and the carts go up another," I said. "It's so cool."

"I know," Ty said.

"It's like a conveyor belt, lifting the carts up-up-up," I said.

"I know," Ty said.

"He *knows*," Sandra said. "We *all* know, because we've all been to Target, including you. Why are you suddenly so fascinated with the stupid escalators?"

"Sandra said 'stupid,'" Ty tattled.

"Sandra," Mom warned. "We don't use that word, remember?"

"I don't know, I just like them," I said. "Nobody else has them, not even the mall. Not even Kmart or Wal-Mart."

"Because at the mall you don't use shopping carts," Sandra said in a duh-voice. "And Kmart and Wal-Mart aren't two stories."

"They built that particular Target in a part of the city that was already developed, so they had limited space to work with," Dad said. "That's why it's two stories."

I scooped up a slurp of shaved ice, reliving the escalator moment in my head. "I was like, 'Bye-bye, Sno-Kone machine! Bye, syrups! See you in a minute!'"

"Oh my God," Sandra said, rolling her eyes. She stood up and took her cup to the counter. "I've got homework to do."

"And I want to read the paper," Dad announced. I noticed he hadn't finished his Sno-Kone, but he dumped it in the sink before I could alert him. "Ellen, would you care to join me?"

"Absolutely," Mom said. She rose from the table. "Winnie? Remember your promise?"

She meant the Sno-Kone machine and how it was my responsibility to clean it. "Yeah, yeah, yeah," I said. "You kids go on. Enjoy yourselves."

She laughed and messed up my hair as she left the room. I was glad things were normal between us again. I hated it when they weren't, even when I was the one causing the problem. Especially if I was the one causing the problem.

"So," I said when it was just Ty and me.

He tilted his cup to get the dregs of his Sno-Kone. The skin around his mouth was red. "I told Taffy about the boy with the steel head," he said.

"What?" I said.

"What you told me, about how he probably grew up to be a criminal."

Uh-oh, my stomach told me. Thank goodness no one else was in the kitchen.

"I told her about the steel plate, too," Ty said.

"And . . . what did she say?"

"That I could have the rest of her pizza."

"Oh."

"I turned the pizza sauce into spit and spitted it into my milk carton."

"Ewww. Did you pour it on anyone?"

Ty looked intrigued, which told me he hadn't.

"Never mind," I said quickly. "So . . . are you and Taffy friends now?"

Ty considered. "She is not my friend, but she's not my enemy."

"Huh." That sounded pretty good, actually. I was impressed.

"Can I see your new bras?" he asked.

"I've got to clean up the kitchen," I said.

"But after?"

"I suppose."

"And can I try one on?"

"Sure," I said, feeling generous. "We'll try them on together."

June

GRADUATION, GRADUATION, GRADUATION. By the last week of school, that was all anyone could talk about. Our ceremony was this coming Friday, and we were all going to dress up, and there'd be musical numbers and speeches and a PowerPoint presentation called "Then and Now," which the office lady, Pam, put together each year. I knew the format from other graduations, although this year we'd be the ones whose cute little baby pictures would be shown, followed by pictures of us in our sixth-grade glory. I wondered what songs Pam would choose for the sound track. Last year, one of the background songs was "Sing a song. Make it simple, to last your whole life long!" At the la-la-la-la-la part, everyone in the auditorium joined in. It made my heart swell, even though I wasn't one of the kids moving on.

This year, I was. Bye bye, elementary school; hello, junior high. Yikes—I wasn't ready to think about that. So I didn't. I filed into the gym with the rest of Mr. Hutchinson's class for a special Tuesday-morning assembly, and we took our seats up front with the other sixth graders, facing out toward the rest of the students.

Mrs. Daly, our principal, asked for everyone's attention. As she spoke, I looked at the scramble of cross-legged younger kids, searching for Ty. There sure was a lot of squirming going on. Had we been that squirmy when we were in the lower grades? Some of us were, no doubt. Alex Plotkin, who was even now sneakily trying to pick his nose with the old "it's just an itch" technique, had definitely been a squirmer.

I found Ty with the rest of the kindergartners. He waved shyly, as if he was in awe of me and my singled-out, sixth-grade status. I felt tender toward him. My own kindergarten year was impossibly distant, as distant in one direction as college was in the other.

This was what was real, this moment right now, even though it had a feeling of unrealness. We were on the verge of something big. It was coming whether we wanted it to or not.

"And now," said Mrs. Daly, "we'd like to carve out some time to honor our very special sixth graders, who will be graduating in three days."

Hoots and whistles filled the air. Mrs. Daly made a settle-down motion, but in a good-humored way. "Each sixth grader will be asked to stand up, and the rest of you will have a chance to share memories about that particular student. Let's keep it to three memories per person so that we have time for everybody. Louise, let's start with you."

Louise, who was sitting on the far left of the semicircle,

stood up looking embarrassed, but I knew it was just because she was the first one to go. Her eyes flew hopefully to the audience.

A third grader raised her hand. "I remember that Louise won the spelling bee two years in a row," she said. "She is a very good speller."

Louise beamed.

"I remember Louise for always using me as an armrest," said a fourth grader named Terrence. Everyone laughed, because that was Louise in a nutshell. She was always using people as armrests.

"How about one more," Mrs. Daly said. She scanned the group. "Yes, Karen?"

"I remember Louise for being a good friend," Karen said, her voice trembling over the words. Someone always said that about each sixth grader, usually his or her best friend. It was boring, but sweet. Louise leaned over and hugged Karen, who was teary, and everyone went "Awww."

Next Karen stood up, wiping her eyes with the back of her hand. People remembered her for giggling a lot, which made her giggle, and for loving chocolate milk, which also made her giggle. Louise remembered her for being a good friend, and once again came the chorus of "Awwww."

Alex Plotkin was remembered for being obsessed with udders, which was an extremely strange comment and one I didn't care to contemplate. Sheila Murphy was remembered for giving a fifth grader a Native American dreamcatcher.

Maxine Rubenstein was remembered for being a good book partner, only not really, because the first grader who said it meant it about Sheila instead. So then a bonus person was called on for Maxine, who said that Maxine once lent her a pen. *Well whoop-de-do,* I thought. I sure hoped I'd be remembered for more than loaning out pens.

"Winnie," Mrs. Daly said when it was my turn. She regarded me kindly. I knew she liked me, because she liked all the kids.

I rose from my chair. I tried to look pleasant and modest.

A second grader named Cody raised his hand. I had no idea what he was going to say, because I barely knew him.

"Yes, Cody? What do you remember about Winnie?" Mrs. Daly asked.

"One time I fell on the playground and I got hurt and she helped me," he said. "And I felt better after that."

"Oh, that's so sweet," someone said. Amanda, of all people. She was sitting five seats down, and when our eyes met, she smiled. Surprised warmth spread through me.

"She is the fastest in the whole school at climbing to the top of the swing set," said a fifth grader named Anna. *Why yes, I am,* I thought. I didn't know anyone had noticed.

Dinah raised her hand. "I will always remember Winnie, because she is the very best friend in the whole entire universe," she said proudly.

"Awww," said everyone.

I gave her a hug, and I meant it, but I wished the remembrances could have gone on and on. I wished they hadn't stopped at three.

For the rest of the day, everyone was in high spirits.

"See what happens when we say nice things about each other?" Mr. Hutchinson said, once we were back in our classroom. "This is how to achieve world peace. Just get everyone together and be kind to one another!"

"I agree," said Dinah, who'd been praised for being an expert at Chinese jump rope and for making up cool dance moves, as well as for being a good friend to a certain Winifred S. Perry. When I said it out loud, it was like, *Well, here goes nothing.* And then it didn't turn out to be as hard as I'd thought.

"Blessed are the cheese makers—I mean *peace* makers," Mr. Hutchinson said, making one of his random corny jokes. "And now, on with life. Take out your math books, please, and get to work on your fractions."

On the playground, everyone continued to be nice. Even Gail was less eye-rolly than normal when Dinah said how much she was going to miss the teachers because they were so full of love.

"The whole school is full of love," Dinah proclaimed with a painfully earnest expression.

A month ago, a remark like that would have meant instant ridicule. *The whole school is full of love?* But after graduation everyone was going their separate ways, and we knew it. I would start seventh grade at Westminster, as would Amanda and Dinah and Louise. And—ugh—Gail. But Maxine and Sheila would be going to Pace Academy, and Chantelle and Cara were going to Lovett. And Karen, Louise's best friend, was moving to Alaska, which meant we'd probably never see her again.

How crazy, to know someone and go to school with her, and then have her be gone from your life forever.

Maxine started sniffling. "I'm not sure I want to graduate," she said.

"Me neither," said Chantelle. "I'm going to miss everyone so much!"

"And the teachers!" Dinah said.

"And the playground!" Cara said.

"And the water fountain where Robert almost kissed me!" Amanda said.

"I don't want to move!" wailed Karen. "Even if I do get to have moose in my backyard!"

"People, people!" I cried. I pulled great clumps of my hair. "Will the madness never end?!"

It made everyone laugh, which was my goal, because it was either that or cry. I noticed that Amanda looked especially amused, and at the same time I noticed myself noticing. Sometime over the last couple of months, I'd fallen out of the habit of seeking her attention, but here I was doing it again. Was it because of her "how sweet" remark during the morning assembly?

She grinned at me, like *you loon*. And before Mr. Hutchinson called us in for Spanish, she ran over and pulled me away from the crowd.

"Hey," she said, "are you busy tonight?"

"I don't know," I said. "Why?"

"There's this lady coming to my house to talk about summer camp. We're having, like, a tea for her. Want to come?"

"Uh . . . sure," I said. "I mean, I'll have to check. But sure." Why was I suddenly so tongue-tied?

"Bring your mom," Amanda said. I'd forgotten how pretty she was, with her sprinkling of dusty freckles. "Bring Dinah, too, if you want. That would be totally fine."

"Okay," I said.

Mr. Hutchinson blew his whistle, and she squeezed my arm and dashed off.

"I don't understand why she waited so long to invite you," Mom said, grumpy at missing her TV show even though I set up the VCR to tape it for her.

"I don't know, because she was busy," I said.

"It's not the most convenient of times," Mom said. "Sandra's volleyball banquet is tomorrow, and I'm supposed to bring refreshments, which means I need to bake a couple dozen cookies. And I still haven't hemmed your graduation dress."

I eyeballed her. She maintained her indignation for a moment, then laughed, knowing she'd been called out. Like she'd really be hemming my graduation dress instead of mooning over the cute gardener on her show.

At Amanda's house, the camp presentation had already started. Mom joined the other parents in the cluster of chairs and sofas, and I scurried onto the floor beside Amanda. Some of the girls I didn't know. They were probably from Amanda's neighborhood and didn't go to Trinity. But I saw Maxine leaning against the coffee table, and Louise was sitting next to her. I gave a small wave. They waved back. Mysteriously, there was no sign of Gail.

Mrs. Foskin, the camp lady, talked for a bit about Camp Winding Gap, then dimmed the lights for a slide show. We saw girls doing farm chores, girls paddling canoes, girls with their arms around one another in front of their cabin. They looked so happy. We saw girls eating dinner in a big room with rows of long tables. We saw a line of girls on horseback, framed by the setting sun.

I glanced behind me at Mom. She smiled at me, and I smiled back. I imagined myself hiking through the woods and building fires, and on Sundays having church in an outdoor chapel. I imagined myself galloping on a pure white horse, its mane flying in the wind. I'd never ridden a horse, but I'd seen people do it on TV. It didn't look hard.

"Good ol' Lightning," I'd say at the end of a satisfying day. My campmates would gather round as I brushed his silky coat. "We rode out early to see the sunrise, and then we just kept going. What about you guys? You ever ride a horse so fast it felt like flying?"

The lights in the Wilsons' living room came back on. I blinked in surprise.

"Camp Winding Gap is a wonderful, positive, enriching experience," Mrs. Foskin said, clasping her hands in front of her. "And now, I'd be delighted to answer any questions." She lifted her eyebrows to acknowledge a woman in the back. "Yes?"

"How much does it cost?" the woman asked.

Mrs. Foskin explained about two-week sessions versus three-week sessions. Amanda's mom caught Amanda's eye and subtly tilted her head, and Amanda got to her feet. She pulled me up with her.

"It's time for snacks," she whispered. "Come help."

In the kitchen, I fell into my role as if it were second nature. I remembered every little thing about Amanda's house, even though I hadn't been over for months. But when I went to get some napkins, I came up empty. The napkin drawer was full of plastic containers.

"My mom rearranged," Amanda said, coming over and opening the next drawer up. She pulled out a stack of napkins, the good kind that were soft and thick. "Here."

"Mercy buckets," I said, stealing Mom's fake French way of saying "thanks." I started pairing brownies with napkins, arranging them on a tray. "So . . . why isn't Gail here?"

"She already has a summer camp," Amanda said. If she

knew it was hard for me to ask, she didn't show it. "It's for being an equestrian. You know, horses?"

"Oh," I said.

"She goes every year. She's really good."

She would be, I thought. She probably wore those tight black pants and everything. Jodhpurs.

Knowing that Gail was an expert rider made my Lightning fantasy seem stupid, until I rebounded with an encouraging thought. It was quite possible that I had my own horsey talent, hidden until now. This could be the summer to reveal it.

"What about Dinah?" Amanda asked.

"Huh?" I said.

"Why didn't she come tonight? To the slide show?"

"Ohhhh," I said. "Um, spend-the-night camp wouldn't work for her. She'd miss her dad too much. You know."

Amanda nodded understandingly. She made a sound of sympathy for Dinah's long-gone mother.

"They're really close," I said.

The truth was, I hadn't told Dinah about Amanda's invitation. Again, that sense of unrealness washed over me, of everything falling away if I let it.

"Well," Amanda said. "It's probably best."

"Yeah," I said, not sure what I was agreeing with.

On graduation night, I wore my beautiful white dress, and I *felt* beautiful, even with the knowledge of my nude-colored bra pressing into my shoulder blades. Mom had finally gotten around to hemming the one loose thready part, and she'd bought me a pair of white sandals with teeny blue dragonflies where the straps crossed over my toes. I wore my blue flower earrings and felt exquisite from head to toe.

"You look like a fairy," Dinah whispered as we lined up to the right of the stage.

"Don't I?" I replied. I grinned and sashayed my hips. Then I leaned in and said, "You look good, too. I really like your necklace."

"Thanks," she said, blushing. It was so easy to make her happy. It made me happy, making her happy. Tonight was all about being happy.

During the "Now and Then" part of the evening, I watched, rapt, as my sixth-grade life flashed in front of me. Pam had been very sneaky with her camera, catching shots of the Halloween Parade, the Spring Carnival, even student-teacher conferences—with one hilarious picture of an abashed Alex Plotkin being lectured by Mrs. Daly. Most of the pictures showed kids who were smiling, though, and it occurred to me that we looked like the kids at Camp Winding Gap. Just as filled-to-the-brim with life.

I pressed my lips together to keep from sharing my observation with Dinah. Mom had said "we'll see" when I begged her to let me join Amanda at camp, and "we'll see" was a good sign. Graduation plus the possibility of camp with Amanda was an intoxicating mix. I wiggled in my seat.

After the "school life" part of Pam's presentation came

the baby-picture finale. There was rosy-cheeked Maxine, her hair as dark and curly when she was an infant as it was now. And there was Alex Plotkin as a toddler, wearing a diaper and cowboy boots and nothing else. Everyone howled.

Gail's picture showed her in a pink ballerina costume; Amanda, in her photo, was propped precariously against a teddy bear. The teddy bear was bigger than she was. It was so amazing, all these lives. All these lives changing and growing and turning into . . . us.

Dinah's picture was sweet, showing her as a baby nestled under a Christmas tree. She drew a chorus of *awwws*, and I was glad for her. I reached over and squeezed her hand.

My picture was one of the last. I had no idea which one Mom had picked, and I laughed with the others when I saw four-year-old me, looking stern in a trench coat and safety goggles from our dress-up drawer. I remembered pretending to be a spy in that particular outfit.

"That's so *you*!" Louise called.

I hid my face, but of course I loved it.

When the ceremony was over, we were sixth graders no more. We were soon-to-be seventh graders. Soon-to-be junior-highers. We shrieked with the weirdness of it while our parents chatted in the parking lot, and we ran like crazy around the playground. One last glorious free-for-all, like those funny square hats thrown into the sky. Only we were the ones flung topsy-turvy, not knowing where we would land.

July

CAMP WINDING GAP was divided into three cabins: the Chickadees, ages nine to ten; the Hummingbirds, ages eleven to twelve; and the Peregrines, ages thirteen to fourteen. It would have been fun to have been a Chickadee, because that was such a dorky-cool name, as in "Hi, I'm a Chickadee!" or "Hey there, little Chickadee!" But Hummingbirds were cool, too. Even cooler, since Amanda and I were Hummingbirds together. We got to share a bunk bed and everything, me on the top and Amanda on the bottom. We both wanted it that way. We both got our first choice.

"Finish making your beds and then come outside," said our counselor, whose name was Amy. Amy had jet-black hair and a square jaw and big breasts. I guessed her to be around Sandra's age. She was a photographer, and if we wanted we could pick photography as one of our activities. I probably would.

I plumped my pillow with a series of overzealous punches, making the girls around me laugh, then walked with the others outside and sat down on a log. I propped my chin on my hands and made my expression super attentive.

Amy cleared her throat, and I said, "Yesssss?"

The other girls laughed again. It made me tingle and want more.

"*Shhh,*" Amanda said.

"Thank you, Amanda," Amy said. "Now. Who can tell me why we're sitting around the fire ring, but there's no fire?"

"Because no one had any matches?" I suggested. Madison, the girl to my left, snickered.

"No," Amy said.

"Because no one lit the kindling?" I couldn't help it—it was there for the taking. I felt proud of myself for knowing the word *kindling.*

"*No,*" Amy said. Amanda nudged me with her knee.

"Is it for safety reasons?" a girl named Jaden asked. "Like, maybe a fire restriction?"

"No, but good guess," Amy said.

No better than mine, I thought.

"There's no fire," Amy said, "because until today, there have been no campers."

"Ohhhh," I said.

"And without campers, our fire has no life."

"It's a metaphor," I whispered loudly to Madison. "We are the fire! We are the coals that give it new life!"

"Winnie, hush," Amanda said under her breath. "For real."

But I was having too much fun, and I didn't understand why Amanda wasn't equally amused. Amy, too. I gave her my cutest smile, which I stole from Ty, but it had little effect.

With great formality, Amy lit a match from the box she pulled from her pocket. She tossed it into the kindling, and it fizzled out. Several of us tittered. She tried again, and this time one of the twigs caught fire.

"We *are* like the fire," Amy said. "Alone, we're nothing, just random pieces of wood. But together, we burn bright and strong."

"You mean we're going to burst into flames?" I whispered to Madison. "Owwie!"

Amy glared. "Winnie, did you have something you wanted to share with the group?"

Everyone looked at me. I looked back. And then . . .

I farted. A loud one, loud enough to be heard over the popping of the fire. There was a shocked silence, and then Madison said, "She tooted!" My cabin mates, including Amanda, fell into hysterics. I was mortified.

"Fine," Amy said. "Thank you for that, Winnie. But I think we'll stick to fire and take a pass on the natural gas."

The hilarity tripled, and Amy allowed herself a small smile. Amanda put her arm around me as if to comfort me, then drew back and said, "Pewww!"

"Ha ha," I said, face burning.

"Just teasing," she said.

"It's time for Group Sing," Amy said, heaving herself to her feet. "You guys head on to the main lodge."

"What about the fire?" Jaden asked.

"I need one person to stay behind and help me put it out," Amy said. She scanned the group. I thought she was going to pick me, as punishment or reward or some sort of peace treaty, but she didn't. She picked Jessica, a tall girl with red hair pulled back in a ponytail. The rest of us were free to go.

That night, in my new-to-me bunk bed that squeaked when I moved, I felt strange in my own skin. I was so far away from Mom and Dad—that was one weird thing. I was basically sleeping outside—that was another. Yes, we were in a cabin, but the walls were thin and there weren't real windows, just screens. And no electricity, of course. Or running water. To wash up before bed, we'd used the one girls' bathroom at the top of the hill. If I had to use the bathroom in the middle of the night—which I wouldn't, because no way was I going up there alone—I'd be in deep doo-doo.

Deep doo-doo. Ha. Too bad everybody was asleep, or I'd have had another good one for them.

And that was the weirdest thing: this new barrel of laughs I'd somehow become. At home I was funny, sure, but in spurts like everyone else. Or more often, funny to myself but not funny to, say, Sandra. Here, I started out being funny because of nervousness and hyperness, and it had stuck. It had been only one day, but I could feel, because of how camp was, that this wasn't a role I'd be able to shrug off. Even if I wanted to.

I wished I hadn't farted, though. That hadn't been on purpose. Who could fart on purpose, anyway?

Never mind. Half the boys from my class, that's who.

But not me. I wished I could go back and make it so that moment never happened. Not said the bit about bursting into flames, so that Amy wouldn't have put the spotlight on me. Or maybe, if I'd felt the fart coming, I could have fallen backward off the log at the same time, which would have covered the sound and still given people something to laugh at.

Well, what was done was done. If I really was the person I was pretending to be—and who's to say I wasn't? Who's to say that this me wasn't the real me, and the back-home me the fake? But if I *was* that person, the jokey confident one, then I'd laugh over the fart and move on. So that's what I tried to do, as cicadas chirped and darkness wrapped around me and rustlings came from the woods that could have been bears, but probably weren't.

A week into camp, a horse stepped on my foot and wouldn't get off. The horse's name was Pudding Treat, and perhaps this was the reason. Because who names a horse "Pudding Treat"? *Good ol' Lightning*, now that had a noble ring. But *good ol' Pudding Treat*? He was fat and lazy and flies were always buzzing around him. He was as far from my fantasy horse as a horse could be without, in actuality, being a cow.

And he was standing on my foot. And it *hurt*.

"Um, excuse me?" I said, trying to get the instructor's attention. At the same time, I pushed hard against Pudding Treat's massive side. He didn't budge.

The instructor, whose name was Leigh-Ann, kept talking about whatever she was talking about.

"Excuse me," I said louder. Leigh-Ann was out in the middle of the riding ring, and all of us who were taking horseback riding were circled around her with our horses beside us. Or on us, in my case. "Excuse me, but I've got a problem!"

Leigh-Ann broke off. She shielded her eyes from the sun. "Yes, Winnie?"

I fought back tears. "He's on my foot! He's standing on my foot!"

"Oh my God!" Leigh-Ann cried. She dropped everything and ran over. "Move," she said to Pudding Treat, shoving on his foreleg in a way that made his knee buckle. My foot slipped free.

"Let's get that shoe off," Leigh-Ann said, fumbling with the laces of my sneaker. She put her arm around my waist and helped me hobble to the water trough. "Put your foot in there. Why on earth didn't you *tell* me?"

"I did," I said.

"But why didn't you yell? Or scream? Or *something*?"

The other girls gathered around. They all looked concerned.

"You're so brave," Madison said.

"Are you okay?" Jaden said. "Your foot's turning red!"

"Can you wiggle your toes?" Leigh-Ann asked. "Is anything broken?"

I wiggled my toes in the lukewarm water. Everything worked.

"Thank goodness," she said. "But you're done for the day—and next time, if a horse steps on your foot, I want you to *do* something about it." She pushed her bangs out of her eyes. "Girls, I need one of you to take Winnie to the cabin. Who wants to go?"

Everyone raised her hand, and a chorus of "Me, me!" filled the air.

"Amanda," I said.

Amanda stepped forward, proud to be chosen.

"Stop by the lodge and have Alice give her some ibuprofen," Leigh-Ann instructed. Amanda nodded. My foot still throbbed, but it was fun being the patient everyone wanted to take care of.

"The rest of you, back to your spots," Leigh-Ann said. "And keep your feet out from under your horses!"

Back in the cabin, with my foot propped on a pillow, I let Amanda make a fuss over me.

"Eat one of these," she said, handing me a Mike and Ike's HOT TAMALE from the stash in her trunk.

"Ooo, spicy," I said, smushing the candy between my teeth.

"I know I'm not supposed to have them in the cabin—but

oh well," she said. She perched on the edge of my bed. "I can't believe you just *stood* there while Pudding Treat was on your foot. Did it kill?"

"Uh-huh," I said. "But I was too embarrassed."

"I would have been screaming my head off," she said. She shook another handful of HOT TAMALES into my hand. Her expression told me she was going to change the subject. "So . . . who do you think's going to be Miss Hummingbird?"

Miss Hummingbird was like the most popular girl of all the Hummingbirds. There'd also be a Miss Chickadee and a Miss Peregrine. All the cabins voted, and the winners would be announced on the last day of camp.

"I don't know," I said. "Maybe Jessica?" Jessica was the red-haired girl who was so clearly Amy's favorite. I watched Amanda's face and quickly added, "Or you? Maybe you, I bet!"

"No, not me," Amanda said. "I think it'll be you."

"Ha ha," I said.

"No, seriously," she said. "Everybody loves you. It's so weird."

"Hey, now!" I couldn't decide whether to be thrilled at the compliment or put off by Amanda's qualification. I laughed.

"You know what I mean," Amanda said.

"Not really," I said.

Amanda shrugged. "You're different here at camp. I don't know why, but you are."

So she *had* noticed. I had wondered.

"I don't know why, either," I said. "I guess it is sort of weird."

"Good weird, though." She shook out the last three HOT TAMALES and gave one to me and popped the other two into her mouth. "Are you glad you came?"

"I am completely and totally glad I came," I said. "Are you?"

"That I came, or that you did?" she asked.

I kicked her with my good foot.

"Both," she said. "I'm glad of both."

On the last day of camp—or rather the last full day, since the next day our parents would come pick us up—I stood up to the cheers of my cabin as I was proclaimed Miss Hummingbird. Amanda clapped loudest of all. I walked with Miss Chickadee and Miss Peregrine to the front of the lodge, where we picked up the trays of sloppy joes for our tables. Some might have said it was unfair that the most popular girls in each cabin were the ones who had to serve lunch, but I didn't mind. I liked being the server.

I didn't want a sloppy joe, so I made myself a Camp Winding Gap Special instead. Peanut butter always stood on the table, as well as white bread, for those who didn't want the day's entrée. There were also lemon wedges and sugar for the iced tea. To make a Camp Winding Gap Special, you spread peanut butter on a piece of bread, then sprinkled on a spoonful of sugar, then squeezed a lemon over the whole thing. Mmm-mmm.

"My very last Camp Winding Gap Special," I intoned, holding my bread aloft.

"You could make one at home," Madison pointed out. "Do you have lemon juice? Just tell your mom to buy some."

"It wouldn't be the same," I said.

"She's right," Jaden said. Sloppy-joe sauce dotted the corner of her lips. "Last year I made one with one of my school friends, and it *wasn't* the same. It just tasted . . . wrong."

"When camp is over, it's over," Jessica said. "The end."

"But that's so sad!" Madison said.

"That's life," said Jessica.

I'd learned during a late-night gab session that Jessica had had leukemia when she was a kid, so I guess she knew what was life and what wasn't. I admired her for it. Madison, on the other hand, seemed a little spoiled. During that same late-night session, Madison had complained that the one thing she didn't like about camp was having to make up her own bed. Amanda and I had shared a look.

Madison pushed away her sloppy joe. "In that case, I'm having my last Camp Winding Gap Special, too."

"Me, too," said Jaden, reaching for the bread.

"All hail the Camp Winding Gap Special!" I said.

"Will you write me?" Madison said out of nowhere, beseeching me with her eyes.

"Huh?" I said.

"After we leave," she said. "Will you write me? Promise?"

"Sure," I said easily. If that was the price I had to pay for being Miss Hummingbird, then bring it on. I even had my own stationery, which my grandmom had given me and which had wildflowers printed across the pages.

But at the same time, I felt it was my responsibility to cut Madison off before her teariness grew into something bigger. Plus, she was unexpectedly reminding me of Dinah, whom I hadn't thought about the whole time I was here. I remembered Dinah's expression when I told her I was going to Camp Winding Gap. It was the same mix of neediness and abandonment that I now saw in Madison. But I hadn't abandoned Dinah, any more than I'd be abandoning Madison when I drove off with Mom and Dad tomorrow. We were big girls. Like Jessica said, *that's life*.

"We should go skinny-dipping," I announced. Immediately, the mood at the table changed.

"Omigosh, we should," Jessica said.

"I've never been skinny-dipping," Jaden said. "Have you?"

"No, and that's why we should," I said.

Amanda giggled. "I don't think I'm a skinny-dipping kind of girl."

"You can be if you want to be!" I argued. Suddenly this was important. "You can be whoever you want!"

Madison fooled with her Camp Winding Gap Special, drawing a line in the lemony sugar crystals. I could tell she wanted to do it.

"Where would we go?" she asked.

"To the lake, past where we put the canoes in," I said. "That hidden spot by the trees." I stood up, knowing we had to go *now* before anyone chickened out. "Come on!"

The five of us giggled as we left the lodge, trying to act casual.

"Where are you girls going?" Amy asked from the counselors' table.

"Um . . . to check on our arts-and-crafts projects," I improvised.

"Be back in time for your afternoon activity!" she called. "And don't forget—we're doing barges tonight!"

"What does she mean, 'barges'?" I asked Jaden, since this was her third summer. We fast-walked down toward the lake, leading the rest of the pack.

"Those little boats we made out of tree bark," she said. "Remember? We're going to melt candles onto them and float them down the river. It's so pretty."

"Oh," I said. We got to the lake and squelched our way to the tucked-away niche beyond the dock. It wasn't perfectly blocked off from the camp, but pretty much so. The others clumped around us. Amanda was slightly out of breath. She raised her eyebrows, like *are you really going to go through with this?*

"Well . . ." I said. My heart pounded. "Here goes nothing!" I pulled off my shirt and bra and stepped out of my shorts and undies. Quick quick quick, because I was aware

of everyone staring. I splashed into the lake—cold! cold!—
and then I was doing it, skinny-dipping, with water swirling
all about.

"Come on in!" I called. Adrenaline surged through me.
"It's awesome, I swear!"

Jessica hesitated, then peeled off her clothes and plunged
in. Then Jaden, and then Madison, although she kept her
underwear on until she was submerged, and only when she
was fully covered did she toss them onto the bank. She forgot, apparently, that eventually she'd have to get out.

"Amanda!" I cried. "Come *on*!"

"I can't!" she cried. "I'm too much of a wimp!"

"No, you're not," I said. I got stern, to the delight of the
others. "Get in right this second, or you'll regret it for the
rest of your life!"

Amanda took her shirt off, then her shorts. Her undies
matched her bra. Both had pink flowers.

"Can't I just get in like this?" she asked.

"Noooo!" we said.

She gnawed on her thumbnail, her other arm wrapped
around her ribs. Then she turned sideways and slipped off
her undies. Last of all came her bra, and I saw that I'd been
wrong about her not needing one. Crossing both arms over
her chest, she ran squealing into the water.

"*Yes!*" I said when she reached the rest of us. I slapped
her a slippery high five.

A stick-snapping sound came from the bank, and Amy

emerged from the trees. "What in the world is going on here?" she demanded.

Everyone shrieked. It was like at a slumber party, where someone's dad says "Boo" right at the scary part of a movie.

"It's Amy!" Madison cried unnecessarily. "Hide!"

"Where, you dork?" Jessica said. Although even she ducked down to her chin in the water. We all did.

"Whose idea was this?" Amy said. She zeroed in on me. "Let me guess. Winnie?"

I straightened my spine, but kept my chest submerged. "I cannot tell a lie," I said. "It was . . . Amanda!"

"*What?!*" Amanda screeched.

Jessica and Jaden cracked up. Madison snorted out a snot bubble.

"Um, just kidding?" I said. I grinned hopefully.

Amy stayed mean for only a second. "Well, if you can't beat 'em, join 'em," she said, pulling off her rugby. Everyone shrieked again. Her breasts really were ginormous.

She stripped off the rest of her clothes and splashed into the lake, and for once I didn't make jokes about things I shouldn't have, like the bruise above her nipple that looked like a bite mark. I could have said plenty about that. I could have made everybody laugh. But I didn't need to. It was enough, just swimming naked in the water.

That night, I sniffled along with the others as we set our bark boats afloat in the river. First I'd had my last Camp Winding

Gap Special, then my last (and first) skinny-dip in the pond, and now this, the last time I might ever sail a bark boat down Horse Pasture River. It felt familiar, this parade of melancholy "lasts," and I didn't know why. But then I realized. It was like graduation, with its similar string of good-byes.

So much sadness, last month leaving sixth grade and now leaving camp. But this time, while it was true that I was losing something, I'd also gotten something back: Amanda. I wouldn't say it out loud. I didn't need to. Still, it was a gift that had dropped down from the sky. We both needed a reminder of how great we were, that's all.

Anyway, this was a happy sort of sadness, a sadness to sink into and enjoy. The candles on our boats flickered as they set off on their journeys, and our voices filled the air with wistful song. *"Silently flows the river to the sea, and the barges, too, go silently. Barges, I would like to go with you, I would like to sail the ocean blue."*

August

THE COOL THING ABOUT AMANDA, as opposed to Dinah, was that Amanda didn't always let me be the leader. With Dinah, I was the one who'd say what we would do, and then we'd do it, and it would be fun, because I *was* a genius with such things. And I liked how Dinah would giggle and make me feel brilliant, like the time we attached a fishing line to a tangerine and flushed it down the toilet, then tugged it back out again. Now that was high entertainment. And gross. But mainly high entertainment.

Amanda, on the other hand, shot my ideas down when she thought they were stupid. Then she'd suggest ideas of her own, which was how we started hanging out at the trampoline. It was originally Amanda and Gail Grayson's secret place, but Gail was at equestrian camp and therefore out of the picture. Anyway, it wasn't as if I barged in without permission. Amanda led me to the trampoline herself, hidden in the woods behind the Graysons' condominium complex. She knew I'd appreciate it, and I did. A secret trampoline, rusty and abandoned, with one big hole in the corner that you had to stay away from. But other than that, absolutely perfect.

"How did you find this place?" I asked, timing my words to match my bounces. I loved how free I felt, like an astronaut springing across the moon.

Amanda bounced across from me, going up when I went down and down when I went up. That way we got maximum jumpability.

"Gail and I were just out exploring one day," Amanda said. "We don't know why it's here, or who left it. And I'm sure my mom would think it's dangerous, so don't say anything."

I rolled my eyes. Like I'd be that stupid.

"Too bad Gail can't be here with us, huh?" I said. I didn't mean it, but I wanted to try out the possibility of being generous. Or maybe I was hoping for more. Maybe I wanted Amanda to look puzzled and say, *Who?* Or if not that, at least, *Nah, it's better with just us.*

Instead Amanda said, "Oh, I know. I miss her so much. First I was at camp, and now she is. Is that totally unfair or what?"

"Totally," I mumbled. I bounced high, then dropped to my knees, then back to my feet. "Try that," I said.

"Easy," Amanda said, copying me without a struggle. "Try this." She dropped to her knees, then bounced and landed on her butt, then bounced back to standing. I tried, but my bounce wasn't high enough to get back off my butt.

"Just as I suspected," Amanda said.

"Oh, please. You've practiced way more."

Amanda showed off, doing a knee-drop followed by a flip. She grinned.

I grinned back. I didn't care that she was better than me. I was just happy to be hanging out with her. Would Dinah be able to do a knee-drop-flip? I don't think so. And maybe it wasn't nice to think that way, because as Mom said, you couldn't compare apples and oranges. And maybe I liked both. Maybe I was an applange. Or an orpple. Or maybe— okay, fine—the two didn't really mix.

Whatever. Bouncing on the trampoline I felt weightless, just the way I liked it.

"Mom, can I ride bikes with Amanda?" I asked the next day.

"Winnie, you've played with Amanda every single day this week," Mom said. "Not that I have anything against Amanda. You know I love Amanda. But don't you think you should spend some time with Dinah?"

I groaned, taking issue with everything Mom said. First of all, Amanda and I did not "play." We hung out. And second of all, why bring Dinah into it? That only complicated things.

"Why don't you invite her to join you two?" Mom said. "Amanda's a sweet girl. I'm sure she would understand."

I groaned louder. The fact that she'd have to understand said it all.

"Mom, Amanda invited *me*, not Dinah," I said. "We're

biking to the—" I stopped myself. I almost said, "trampoline," but changed it at the last second. "Drugstore. We're going to look at lip gloss."

"Since when have you started caring about lip gloss?" Mom said.

"We start seventh grade in less than two weeks," I reminded her. "Seventh graders wear lip gloss, okay?"

"Okay," Mom said, amused. "But Dinah's starting seventh grade, too. Doesn't she need lip gloss?"

"She already has some," I said. "She has tons."

Mom came over to me in the kitchen. She ran her hand through my hair. "Listen, bug. I just don't want you to get hurt, all right?"

I looked at her like she was nuts. What was she talking about?

"You and Amanda, spending so much time together. I'm worried she might let you down again."

I blushed, although I wasn't sure why. "That was last year. We're older now."

"I know," Mom said. "And I also know that I've got to let you make your own mistakes."

"Ex*cuse* me?"

"Just . . . oh, I don't know. Just call Dinah, will you?"

"I called her yesterday," I said.

"You called during her dance lesson. Call her when you know she's going to be there."

What, she was a mind reader now?

"Fine," I said.

"Great," Mom said. She handed me the phone.

"And then can I meet Amanda?"

"Yes, then you can meet Amanda," Mom said.

I punched in Dinah's number. I heard four rings, and then the answering machine picked up. Dinah's voice in the message sounded super young.

"Hi, Dinah," I said after the beep. "It's me. Winnie. Um, call me, okay? Bye!"

I pressed the OFF button.

"She wasn't there, and it's not my fault," I told Mom.

"Oh, Winnie," she said. She cupped my face with her hands, and I made myself hold still for it. "You know . . . Dinah may not always be there for you when you come back."

I pulled away. I'd let her be motherly for *that*?

"Duh, because she's at her piano lesson," I said. I saw Mom's frown and quickly added, "*Probably*. And afterward, she usually goes out to eat with her dad. So?"

"That's not what I mean, and you know it."

I sighed. "Can I just go now? Please?"

"Go," Mom said. "Have fun. Just remember to be careful."

Sitting cross-legged on the trampoline, far from the jagged hole, Amanda and I chomped on Mike and Ike's and traded seventh-grade horror stories. The girl who got her period in the middle of math (wearing a yellow dress!); the girl who showed up with a pair of underwear stuck by static cling to the back of her pants (her mother's underwear at that); the girl who was forcibly held down while two other girls shaved her eyebrows off.

"*Why*?" I said.

"Who knows?" Amanda said. "But it's true. It happened to the daughter of one of my mom's friends. The mean girls told her she should wax because her eyebrows were hairy, but she didn't. So they invited her to a slumber party, and she was all excited because she thought, 'Oh good, I'm finally in their group.' And then they held her down and shaved her eyebrows off."

"That's *terrible*," I said. I passed the Mike and Ike's to Amanda and drew my knees to my chest. Stories like these made me want to stay in elementary school forever. Seriously. And Mom was worried about me being with Amanda? She was crazy.

"What'd she do?" I asked. "The shaved-eyebrow girl."

"I don't know. Probably switched schools—I would."

"But then you wouldn't be with me anymore," I said.

"If I was eyebrowless, I wouldn't want to be with anyone," she said.

"Still," I said. I worked at a bit of candy with my tongue. "Anyway, that would never happen. And the reason it'll never happen is because we *will* be together. Right? I would never let anyone shave your eyebrows off."

"Thanks," Amanda said. "But my eyebrows aren't the slightest bit bushy. My mom says that's lucky, because I'll never have to pluck."

"You've talked about plucking your eyebrows?" I said.

She looked at me, like *you haven't?*

It caught me off guard, this feeling of being one step behind even with someone I'd known all my life.

"I wish Gail would get back from camp already," Amanda said wistfully.

My heart twinged. *I* was the one who'd made a point of bringing her Mike and Ike's, not missing-in-action Gail.

"What, I'm not good enough?" I joked.

She snorted. "Right, you're not good enough. You're just a replacement until she comes home." She flopped back on the trampoline. "Come on . . . don't you miss Dinah?"

"Why would I miss Dinah? She's not out of town."

"Oh," Amanda said. It was obvious she was surprised.

"I just called her this very day," I said, feeling as if I had to go on.

"Well . . . good," Amanda said. "I like Dinah."

"I do, too," I said.

"I know."

"I know you know."

This was dumb. I hopped off the trampoline. I liked Amanda *and* I liked Dinah—was that so hard to understand? Did we have to go through all this again, just when we'd refound each other? Maybe this was what Mom meant when she said she didn't want me getting hurt. Maybe, secretly, Mom knew I wanted Amanda to like me better than she liked Gail, just as maybe, secretly, I liked Amanda better than Dinah.

I think.

Sometimes I did, even though Dinah and I had fun in a way that never left me feeling stranded.

But seventh grade would be easier with Amanda by my side; harder with Dinah. That much I knew. Dinah would be the one, if it fell upon anyone, who got de-eyebrowed. Which would be terrible! That's not what I wanted at all.

All of a sudden I wasn't sure *what* I wanted, and I started back toward the condominium complex. In my confusion, I headed in the wrong direction.

"That's not the way," Amanda said from the trampoline. "What are you doing?"

"I'm taking a shortcut," I said.

"To *where*?" Amanda called. "You're not leaving, are you?"

I didn't answer, just pressed on ahead. I was tangled up inside myself. Maybe people sometimes got hurt—or hurt each other—without it being on purpose. But did that mean you should just . . . walk away from it all? I felt in some unclear way like that wasn't the answer. I also, for no good reason, felt mad at Amanda. Like I needed to get away from her and forge my own path.

I pushed through a dense bushy area. When I felt the first

sting, I thought it was a branch scraping my forearm. Then came another, and another—darts of fire all over my body.

"Help!" I screamed. I pitched forward, trying to escape the jabs on my shins, my thighs, my back. I heard Amanda behind me, her voice pitched high, but the cloud of yellow jackets made it hard to move or even think. "Amanda! Help!"

The yellow jackets droned around me. One stung my cheek, and it hurt so bad I thought I would faint. Another stung the side of my mouth, and I gagged. I felt its body against my lip, fuzzy and hard, and it left me light-headed.

Fingers grasped my upper arm. "Move, Winnie!" Amanda commanded. "You've got to move!"

I turned and staggered toward her. I hardly remember getting to the path, and I hardly remember Amanda pounding on the door of Mrs. Grayson's condominium. I do remember being herded into the front seat of Mrs. Grayson's silver Lexus, because I thought, *She's still got that fake tan* and *Whoa, her perfume is strong.* I also remember how fat my lower lip grew, swelling like one of Ty's microwaved marshmallows. And I remember the taste of salt when I touched it with my tongue. Salt and a sticky sweetness, left over from the Mike and Ike's.

"Tell me again how scared you were for me," I said. We were sitting side by side on my bed, me under the covers and her on top.

"So so *so* scared!" she said. "I was like, 'Poor Winnie! I would have collapsed right there on the spot!'"

"I practically did," I said. "Dr. Harper said it was a good thing I wasn't allergic, or I might have died." It was a dramatic thing to say, but true, and as I watched Dinah's eyes go wide, I felt a welling of love. I'd almost chosen Amanda over Dinah *again*, when it was clear that I wasn't Amanda's first choice at all.

After Mom and I had gotten home from the Youth Clinic, and after Ty had counted all thirty-two of my stings to make sure I wasn't exaggerating, I'd asked Mom for the phone so I could call Amanda. I figured she'd be worried sick.

But before I could tell Amanda anything, her other line beeped. "One sec," she said. Then, when she came back, she said, "Winnie, I am so sorry. It's Gail, and she only gets this one chance every day to use the phone. I'll call you right back, I promise!"

But she didn't. Two hours ticked by, and her call never came.

So I called Dinah, without Mom having to tell me to. Steady, loyal Dinah, who made her dad chauffeur her over right away with a bag of my favorite chocolate-covered pretzels from Whole Foods.

"Well, I am so glad you *didn't* die," Dinah said now. "I can't even imagine if you died." She was struck by a thought. "Oh my gosh. If you died, we wouldn't be able to go to seventh grade together! I'd be all alone!"

"Don't worry," I said, patting her arm. I felt woozy from the pain medication. "I didn't, and you won't. Be alone, that is. You goof!"

She giggled and leaned against the pillow. She touched her toe to mine. "Back to the dramatic reenactment. You ran into the yellow jackets' nest, and you were stung five zillion trillion times . . . and then what?"

"And then a hand reached out through the blur of burning pain"—I made my hand descend from above—"and snatched me from the jaws of death."

"Amanda?"

"She got stung three times. But I got stung thirty-two."

"I know. You told me," Dinah said.

"And now I'm telling you again."

Dinah touched one of my welts, her fingers as light as a moth. She hesitated, then said, "Don't you think it's weird? That she's not here with you now?"

"Who? Amanda?"

She looked at me, like *who else?*

I almost defended Amanda—she was busy, she only got that one call from Gail a day—and then I just . . . *poof*, let it go in my mind.

"I guess it is," I said.

"It's not very cool," Dinah said. It sounded strange coming from her, the word *cool*.

"No," I said, giving the point to Dinah squarely and soundly. "Not cool at all."

I thought about what Mom had said, about how Dinah might not always be there when I came back. But Dinah hadn't even known I was gone. At least, I didn't think she had.

I looked at Dinah as if from a high-up place. I wanted to tell her how enormous it was, this realization of who my friends were and who I myself wanted to be. Amanda wasn't evil, and she'd probably always be in my life. She'd probably always be someone I secretly admired.

But Dinah was here beside me, and I was immensely grateful. Because it could have gone the other way. I'd had a very narrow escape.

"From the yellow jackets?" Dinah said.

Whoa. *Did I just say that out loud?*

"Um, yeah," I said. "The yellow jackets, the world . . . everything."

I offered her a chocolate-covered pretzel, and she happily took three.

September

OKAY, SEVENTH GRADE WAS HUGE. Freakily huge. And not as in tons of people—although there were—but as in, *whoa, big life moment, everything's different and I can't deal.*

"Too bad, because you have to," Sandra said as she drove us to Westminster on the morning of our second day. She shifted into fourth gear, and her lips curved into a barely there smile. She always smiled like that when she changed gears, because she was proud of herself for being so smooth. She'd used her summer savings to buy an old, beat-up BMW, and one of its selling points was that it had a manual transmission. "So many girls don't even know how to drive a stick shift," she'd said to me sternly. "Don't let that be you."

I wouldn't—*if* I ever made it to sixteen. But manual versus automatic was so not my problem right now.

"You don't understand," I said. "I truly can't handle it—and I'm not being dramatic. Yesterday I saw a guy get pantsed in PE, and—"

"For real?" Sandra said, glancing over at me. "You *saw* this?"

"Well, no, but I heard about it," I said. "And they gave this other guy a full-frontal wedgie! They hung him up on a towel hook!"

"Urban legends," Sandra said, dismissing my reports with a wave of her hand. "Nobody at Westminster has ever been hung up on a towel hook, I promise you." She flicked her blinker and turned into Westminster's back gate. To our right was the wooded trail the cross-country runners trained on; to our left were the back tennis courts. There was a second set of tennis courts out by the front gate, along with a rifle range and a ropes course. The place was huge.

I scrunched low in my seat. "But . . . nobody knows me."

"So? You're a seventh grader. Nobody's supposed to know you."

"Gee, thanks. Thanks for being such a great big sister."

"I'm letting you ride with me, aren't I?"

"Only because you have to."

Westminster went all the way through high school, so of course Sandra and I rode together. It only made sense. Westminster had an elementary school as well, up on the hill where the cross-country trail led. But none of us had attended the elementary school, because we went to Trinity. Trinity was nice. Trinity was small. At Trinity, everyone knew me.

Sandra pulled into the girls' parking lot. She cut the engine and yanked up the emergency brake. Then she looked at me, a look that was for real. "Just act confident, even if you're not," she said.

Easy for her to say. She was a junior, and she was sassy and tough and drove a golf ball–yellow Beemer. Plus she was beautiful in her "I'm not trying only secretly I am" kind of way. Plus she was dating Bo.

I sighed. I didn't get out of the car.

Sandra slammed her door. There was no point in locking it, since it was so old. Dad had suggested we wear our bike helmets to stay safe. "Ha ha," we had said.

"I'm leaving," Sandra said, taking a token step toward the part of the campus where she spent her day. "You're going to look really stupid sitting in there by yourself."

I gazed at her plaintively.

"What, you'd rather be homeschooled?" she said.

"Yes," I said.

She strode back and tugged me out of the car. "Go," she said, pushing me toward the junior high. "You're going to be fine. You really and truly are."

In Mrs. Potter's homeroom, which consisted of only girls because the boys had their own homerooms, I sat next to a girl with pink braces named Malena. Next to Malena sat Gail Grayson. Malena had honest-to-God boobs just like Gail, and apparently that was enough to bind the two of them in snobby aloofness. They talked to each other, but neither talked to me. Gail acted as if she didn't even know my name.

Amanda was in Mr. Gossett's homeroom, and Dinah was in Ms. Myzchievich's homeroom. Dinah said she told them to call her Ms. M. Louise was in Ms. M's homeroom, too, and Dinah said she seemed lost without Karen, who was off in Alaska. I felt lost without Dinah, and she was only two rooms down.

Mrs. Potter expected us to be quiet during homeroom and do some sort of work, so I read my history textbook. At Trinity, history had been called "social studies," and our textbooks had been more like workbooks, with color pictures and lists of vocabulary. This year my history book was the size of a dictionary, and its print was just as small. It made me feel grown-up. But it was also really heavy.

Two seats behind me, a girl tapped a message into her cell phone, and Mrs. Potter glanced up from her stack of papers. Uh-oh. We'd been told expressly that cell phones weren't allowed. Not that I had a cell phone, but lots of kids did.

"Ansley, may I ask what you're doing?" Mrs. Potter said.

"Sorry, Mrs. Potter," Ansley said, snapping shut her phone.

"Why aren't you doing something productive?" Mrs. Potter asked.

Ansley's cheeks reddened, probably because everyone was staring at her. And probably because she didn't expect Mrs. Potter to make such a big deal out of it. "Um . . . I don't have a pencil."

"You don't have a pencil," Mrs. Potter repeated. "As I recall, you didn't have a pencil yesterday, either. Do you think, perhaps, a pencil would be a good thing to bring to school?"

"Yes, ma'am," Ansley said.

"Bring me your phone, please," Mrs. Potter said.

Ansley slid out of her seat and walked to the front of the room, where she placed her phone on Mrs. Potter's desk. Mrs. Potter dropped it neatly into the top drawer.

"I suggest you find someone who will lend you a pencil, and I suggest that tomorrow you come prepared," Mrs. Potter said. She waited, then said impatiently, "You may return to your seat."

"But . . ." said Ansley. I knew she was thinking of her phone.

"Yes?" Mrs. Potter said.

Ansley hovered for another moment, then went back to her desk. As she passed, I saw she was fighting back tears. Mrs. Potter didn't seem to care, which was mean. It made me not like her—in fact, it made me feel something hot and sharp toward her—and I didn't like feeling that way toward my teacher.

I also felt scared of her. I didn't like that, either.

I thought longingly of Mr. Hutchinson, who never would have taken anyone's phone or made a federal case out of a missing pencil. If someone forgot her pencil, he gave her one from his stash, simple as that.

A lump rose in my throat. I bowed my head over my work.

During history, I dropped my textbook on the floor and it was extremely loud and Mr. Fackler thought I did it on purpose. During pre-algebra I stepped on some guy's backpack, and he glared in a way that made my heart pound. It was like he thought I was an absolute idiot. For the whole rest of the class I dwelled on it, telling myself, *I stepped on his backpack, that's all. He needs to chill!* But it didn't ease my shame, which even I realized was too big for my crime.

During English everyone snickered when I pronounced *plethora* wrong, even Louise, who should have stuck up for me since she knew me from before. During lunch she tried to make amends by offering me her brownie, but it was too little, too late. If she was going to be nice to me, she'd have to be nice to me all the time, not just when she didn't have anyone to sit with.

By the time Mom picked me up outside the junior high building, I was ready for a heaping dose of motherly love. I told her all about my horrible day, expecting sympathy, but instead I got another version of Sandra's "deal with it" speech from this morning.

"Oh, sweetie," Mom said. "You're going to have an awfully long year if you don't find a way to change your attitude."

So not helpful. I almost wished I'd waited to ride with Sandra, but she had track from four till six. I yearned to veg in front of the TV with a bag of Doritos, not sit in the bleachers and watch Sandra run.

"Why don't you like your school?" Ty asked from his booster seat in the back.

"Because everyone's mean," I said. "You better appreciate

elementary school while you can, because you're going to hate junior high."

"Winnie," Mom chided.

"I love first grade," Ty said. "For snack they gave us Goldfish, and I snuck some in my pocket. Want one?"

"I suppose," I said. I extended my hand from the front seat.

"With tail or without?"

"Uh . . . with, I guess."

"Okay," he said. He made it swim toward me, saying "swim, swim, swim" to clarify the process. Then he jabbed me with it, hard.

"Ow!" I cried. "What'd you do that for?"

"With their tail they hurt more, because they whack you," Ty explained. He waved the Goldfish. "Here."

"I don't want it anymore," I said. To my horror, my voice trembled.

Ty panicked, as he always did when he upset me.

"Winnie, I'm sorry!" he said. "I did not *mean* to whack you!" His fist, grubby with cracker dust, thrust itself into my vision. "Here, you can have all of them. And if they whack you, I will crunch them with my sharp, sharp teeth!"

"I don't want them," I said.

Ty hyperventilated.

"Winnie, tell your brother it's okay," Mom said. "Ty, it's okay. Winnie's not mad at you, are you, Winnie?"

"I am," I said.

"No, you're not," Mom said, pulling up short at a red

light. "Ty, she's not. She's just had a hard day." She looked at me from the driver's seat. "Is there something going on you haven't told me?"

Oh, so *now* she wanted to talk, now that I no longer did. Everything was bad and wrong, and maybe it wasn't Ty's fault, but he sure hadn't helped. It actually felt kind of good to have someone else be unhappy, too.

"Winnie?" Mom said.

"A girl called Dinah the B-word," I said.

"To *Dinah*?" Mom said.

"And all Dinah had done was try to open that other girl's locker by mistake," I said.

"What's the B-word?" Ty asked.

The light turned green, and Mom pressed on the accelerator. "It's something people say when they're not being very nice."

"It rhymes with *witch*," I said. "Only it starts with B."

"*What* rhymes with *witch*?" Ty asked.

I started to answer, but Mom cut me off.

"Never mind," she said. "It's a grown-up word. It's a word we don't use."

"Like *stupid*?"

"Like stupid."

"But Dinah's not stupid," Ty said.

"No, she's not," Mom said.

We rode the rest of the way home in silence.

• • • • • • • • • •

The next day, Dinah stayed home sick, only I didn't think she was *really* sick. She didn't want to face the B-word girl, that's what I thought. I didn't blame her. I wouldn't, either. But that left me all alone in the universe, and in PE, which was the one class I had with Dinah, I felt especially stupid. We were supposed to find partners to do sit-ups with, and without Dinah, there was no partner for me.

All around girls paired up, giggling and chatting. I felt like the biggest dork in the world, standing there trying to look unconcerned but privately feeling the onset of a panic attack. I would have even taken Louise for a partner. In a snap I'd have taken Louise. But she wasn't an option, because she wasn't in my class.

"Everyone set?" Coach Swinson said. The girls in pairs spread out on the mats, and I realized that in a few short moments I was going to be standing there by myself with a sign taped to my chest that said SUPER-ENORMOUS LOSER.

And then . . . salvation.

"Want to pair up?" a girl said, nudging my arm with her elbow. She had brown hair and green eyes with long lashes.

"Yeah, sure," I said.

"I'm Cinnamon," she said.

"What?"

"Cinnamon," she said. "I know it's weird, but that's my name." Her expression—part martyred, part amused—said she'd been through this countless times before.

"Your name is *Cinnamon*?" I said. "That is so cool."

"My parents are pretty hippie-dippy," she explained. She waited, then said, "So . . . do you have a name?"

I blushed. "Oh, right. I'm Winnie."

Coach Swinson clapped her hands. "Let's do it," she said. "I want you each to do as many sit-ups as you can in one minute. Then you'll switch."

Cinnamon and I scrambled into position. She lay on her back with knees bent, and I anchored her feet with my weight. She clasped her hands behind her head.

Coach Swinson blew her whistle. "Go!"

Cinnamon huffed and puffed. Her body jerked beneath me. It was a very intimate thing, holding this newly met person's feet. I focused my attention on counting.

"Fifty-three," I said at the end of the minute. I released Cinnamon's feet, and she extended her legs. She panted, arms spread wide on the mat.

"Time to switch," Coach Swinson said. I lay back and put my hands behind my head, and Cinnamon got into place at my feet.

"Ready, go!"

I strained against her. My stomach muscles did the bulk of the work, but my legs were involved, too, bracing against her grip. Down there on the floor I felt very . . . exposed, and I hoped my shorts weren't gaping at the leg. I also hoped desperately and fervently that there wouldn't be a replay of my fart moment at Camp Winding Gap, because, exerting myself like this, it was entirely possible.

"Fifty-eight, fifty-nine . . . sixty!" Cinnamon cried as Coach Swinson blasted her whistle. "Winnie, that's awesome!"

I grinned, breathing hard. Rather than flopping onto the mat, I rolled onto my side and pushed myself up. Was she mad that I'd done more than her? I didn't think so.

Next came laps around the gym, and Cinnamon fell in beside me even though I didn't expect her to. We chatted as we jogged, and I learned that she was an alpha-omega, which meant she'd started Westminster in pre-K and would assumedly continue on through her senior year. At first I thought, *She must know tons of people—so why'd she pick me? What was wrong with her that left her as partnerless as I was?* Then, more charitably, I decided that maybe it was because she knew so many people that she *did* pick me. Because she was able to, sort of.

I liked her kindness, but I didn't want her pity, so I tried to be witty and entertaining. I told her about Sandra and her ratty BMW and how Dad wanted us to wear bike helmets, which made her laugh. She told me that her own dad had just gotten remarried, and that her new stepmom unfolded Cinnamon's used-up tissues to see how many blows Cinnamon had gotten on them.

"What?!" I said.

"She pulls them out of the trash—I'm not kidding," Cinnamon said. "She's like, 'You're being wasteful by not using the entire Kleenex.' I'm like, 'You're being disgusting by checking!'"

"That's nuts," I said, imagining Cinnamon's stepmom rooting through the garbage. In my mind she wore a velour sweatsuit, like Gail Grayson's mom. Malena, Gail's boob-friend, was in Cinnamon's and my PE class, and she bounced along ahead of us in her green-and-white gym uniform.

"Hey," I said, jerking my chin in Malena's direction. "Do you know that girl?"

"Malena?" Cinnamon said. "She's been here since pre-K, too. Not my favorite."

I was delighted to hear this, and my impression of Cinnamon went up. "Oh yeah? Why?"

"She's not very nice, that's all," Cinnamon said. "I mean—decide for yourself. But, like, she's the kind of girl who makes you feel bad if you suck at field hockey, or whatever. She thinks she's so much better than everyone."

"There's a girl from my old school who's like that," I said, feeling daring. "She goes here now, too. Her name's Gail."

"Great," Cinnamon said. "Just what we need."

I laughed.

In the locker room, I felt happy as I changed back into my normal clothes. I'd made a new friend—maybe—and she was cool. She was also older-acting than my elementary-school friends. And she wore thong underwear. I noticed as she slipped into her jeans.

Still, the very first thing I did when I got home was to call Dinah and tell her she *had* to go to school the next day.

"Because number one, I missed you," I said, "and number two, you're supposed to spend the night tomorrow night, and your dad won't let you if you're supposedly sick." It was one of those rules that all grown-ups seemed to share: if you're sick, you're sick, and there should be nothing fun about it. Even though surely Mr. Devine knew that Dinah had spent all day playing Mario Kart on her GameCube.

"But what if I see that girl again?" Dinah asked. "The one who . . . you know."

"Well, you probably will," I said. "So you might as well go ahead and get it over with."

"I don't want to," Dinah said.

"What other option do you have?" I said. "I mean, come on. Would you rather be homeschooled?"

"Yes," Dinah said.

I switched tactics, because it was all beginning to sound too familiar. "Anyway, what about that dance-group thingie you told me about? The hip-hop club. Don't you want to sign up?"

Dinah was silent. I knew she did, though, because on the first day of school that was all she could talk about. At the time, I hadn't encouraged her, because I wasn't interested in the hip-hop club, and I doubted she'd join without me. But who knows? Maybe she would.

"Plus there's this girl I want you to meet," I went on. "She's in our PE class."

"Oh," said Dinah.

"She's great," I said. "You'll like her, I promise."

And she did. I introduced the two of them the next day, and for just a second I felt worried. Or rather, I felt that old need to apologize for Dinah's . . . Dinah-ness. For the way her gym shorts bunched up around her waist, for the paleness of her thighs.

But Cinnamon smiled at Dinah and said, "Hey." She complimented Dinah's shoes, which had somehow become retro-cool even though they were still her plain old Keds. But if Cinnamon saw them as a statement, who was I to correct her?

Then somehow during battle ball we started barking at one another, like dogs, and it was goofy and fun and made my heart lift. I was a little embarrassed in front of the other girls, especially Maleria, because nobody was barking but us. It *was* a tiny bit elementary-schoolish. But then I was like, *Okay, so we're suddenly cocker spaniels. Is that so wrong? Anyway, Cinnamon started it—and she wears a thong.*

On the walk up the hill from the gym to the junior high building, we pledged that on Monday, we'd all wear our hair in doggy ears, just to be silly.

"And we'll quit wearing makeup," Cinnamon said.

"If we ever wore makeup in the first place, which I don't," I said.

"Yeah -huh," Dinah said. "You wear lip gloss."

"I wear lip *balm*," I said. "Big difference."

Dinah turned to Cinnamon. "Do you wear makeup?" she said. It was the kind of question only Dinah would ask.

"Sometimes," Cinnamon said. She hitched her backpack

higher on her shoulder. "Like, you know, powder on my nose, because it gets shiny. And sometimes sparkle dust on my cheeks."

"I like sparkle dust," I said. I also liked the way she called it *sparkle dust,* when I'd always called it sparkly stuff or sparkles. "I put it on my shoulders."

"But I don't want to be old and boring," Cinnamon said. "I don't want to care what I look like and worry about boys and all that crap."

I thought, *Hmm. Maybe the thong was a fake-out. Or maybe she was worried about seventh grade, too, even though she's been here all along.*

"Well, I'm all for that," I said.

"Me, too," said Dinah.

"Me, three," said Cinnamon.

We gave a triple high five, then laughed when Dinah said "Ow" and shook her fingers.

Mr. Devine let Dinah spend the night since it was clear she was over her mysterious illness. We watched *Dirty Dancing: Havana Nights,* which for some reason Dinah can't get enough of, and scarfed down Jimmy Dean Sausage Biscuits fresh from the microwave. Ty matched us biscuit for biscuit. He also offered fascinating commentary on the movie, such as, "That girl is pretty. I will marry her, and we will live on the moon. Or maybe Atlanta. But not California, because I will not step foot in the Ring of Fire."

"What is he talking about?" Dinah said.

"Nothing," I replied.

Around nine, I kissed Ty good night, and Dinah did, too. He wiped off our slobber, but not the kisses. Then we went upstairs for a little "us" time.

"Ahhhh," I said, falling spread-eagled on my bed. "Our hell week is over!"

"Winnie!" Dinah said, shocked.

I was a little shocked, too. And I immediately felt guilty, because *hell* was a bad word. But mainly I felt giddy, because it was such a relief to be away from junior high for a whole blessed weekend. Even the good parts, like Cinnamon.

Dinah flopped down beside me. The mattress groaned. "It wasn't *all* bad, though," she said. "It wasn't as bad as I'd thought. And next week, the hip-hop club starts! I'm so excited."

"You'll have to teach me your cool moves," I said. "Except I won't be able to do them, because I'm such a klutz."

"I wish you would just sign up," she said.

"Nah," I said. "I'm glad you did, though." I sat up, because even though we'd pigged out on sausage biscuits, I was still hungry. Probably because I hadn't eaten all week. "Hey, do you want a Polar Bar?"

"Ooo, yeah," Dinah said. We loved Polar Bars because of their commercials, which showed people opening their freezers and being blasted by arctic winds as they unwrapped their slabs of ice cream. "Enjoy the Polar Bar Experience," the commercials urged.

We padded downstairs and stood in front of the open freezer with our hair whipping about our faces. Only not really. We took a Polar Bar apiece and scurried back to my room, where we acted out the commercial by taking bites of our ice cream and fainting in chilly delight on the bed.

"The Polar Bar Experience!" I cried, flinging myself backward.

"The Polar Bar Experience!" Dinah echoed. She collapsed beside me with joyful abandon, and the bed crashed to the floor with a bang. We stared at each other in astonishment.

"Mommy, I heard a noise!" Ty cried from his room. His footsteps sounded in the hall, and he burst into my room. "Winnie, why is your bed broken? Why are you and Dinah on the floor?"

Mom and Dad materialized to see what was wrong. Dad's face grew stormy.

"I told you not to jump on the bed," he said.

"No, you didn't," I said in a teeny voice. "Not tonight." When I saw that wasn't working, I said, "Anyway, we weren't jumping on it! We were just . . . lying on it, I promise!"

"Why do you have ice cream?" Ty said, noticing our Polar Bars. "I want ice cream!"

"You brought ice cream to your *room*?" Mom said. Food in our rooms was expressly forbidden, because of roaches that could smell out the least little nibblet of goodness.

"*Winnie*," Dad said. He didn't often get mad, and for just that moment he reminded me of Mrs. Potter, the day she scolded Ansley about her missing pencil.

"I'm so, so very sorry," I said. "It was an accident."

"You accidentally brought ice cream up to your room, and you accidentally jumped on your bed and broke it?" Dad said.

"Uh-huh," I said. And then I couldn't help it. I got the giggles.

Dad's expression darkened, and I knew I should hush and act serious. But tonight Dad's anger didn't have the usual effect. He was scary, there was no denying it, and I knew there'd be consequences galore. But I'd seen—and survived— much worse.

October

"SAY THE WRONG NAME," Louise whispered, leaning across the aisle and breathing into my ear.

"What?"

"When she calls roll. Pass it on."

I glanced at the front of the room. The "she" Louise was referring to was Ms. Braddy, who was subbing for our English teacher, Ms. Duncan, who had the flu. Ms. Braddy was large and smelled like Vaseline, and it was clear from the blinkiness of her eyes that she wasn't the type of sub who knew how to hold her own. Plus, it was the week of Halloween—not a good week for the best of subs. Kids were trying on all sorts of fiendish behaviors, and it wasn't pretty.

Louise kicked my desk. "Pass it *on*."

I leaned forward and told Sydney, who told Malena, who told Ansley, who widened her eyes and nodded before starting it down the next row.

"If I could only find—" Ms. Braddy said to herself. She shuffled again through the papers on the desk, then straightened up with a look of surprise. "Gracious, it's been here all the time." She peered at the attendance sheet. "Sydney LeBey?" she began.

"Actually, I go by Cindy," Sydney said. Malena snorted, and Sydney kicked her shin.

"Cindy," Ms. Braddy said. She made a mark on the sheet. "William Everett?"

"Bill," William said, who never went by "Bill" or even "Will." From the class came a ripple of glee.

"Bill," Ms. Braddy repeated. She moved on down the list. "Malena Willingham?"

"It's *Melanie*," Malena said.

"But it says here—"

"It's a typo."

"Oh. My, I can't get anything right, can I?"

"Nope," William said under his breath. "'Cause you're a *loser*." He stretched the word out the way guys do when they're trying to be funny, and it worked. Everyone laughed. Ms. Braddy grew more flustered.

"Louise Naylor?" she said.

Louise cast her eyes around the room. "Lulu," she said. "I prefer to go by Lulu."

Ms. Braddy did her blinking routine.

"She does," William said. "She goes by Lulu."

"Lulu," Ms. Braddy said aloud. There were titters all around.

By the time it was my turn, there was a faint sheen on Ms. Braddy's wide forehead.

"Winifred Perry?" she called.

Louise looked at me, while to my left Malena smiled with her pink braces. It was the first time she'd ever smiled at me.

"Winifred?" Ms. Braddy said again.

"Uh, Wendy," I blurted. "I go by Wendy."

A noise escaped from behind Sydney's hand, which Ms. Braddy heard.

"The name on the list is Winifred," she said. "I don't believe I've ever—"

"We call her Wendy," Louise interrupted. "We always have."

My face burned. I really didn't need Louise getting into it.

"Well," Ms. Braddy said. "Wendy." Her hands shook as she put the attendance sheet away. "It says here that you're to start off in your workbooks. Is that right?"

"No," Louise said. "Ms. Duncan lets us talk."

"I don't think so," Ms. Braddy said.

"She *does*," Louise said.

"Workbooks," Ms. Braddy said in a too-tight voice. "Begin, please."

By half past the hour, Ms. Braddy had regained her composure. She moved from desk to desk, commenting on "Melanie's" neat penmanship and "Bill's" excellent spelling. She had something nice to say to everyone, and I felt bad for how we'd treated her. She reminded me of my aunt Lucy. Aunt Lucy was a biggish sort of person, too, and at one point she'd been studying to be a teacher. But she'd dropped out of the program, which now I was glad of. Kids could be so mean.

I made a point of raising my hand and answering politely when Ms. Braddy quizzed us on our spelling words, and when she needed someone to come up with a sentence for *unveil*, I was her girl. Louise frowned at me like I was a suck-up, but I tried to ignore her.

The end of the period rolled around, and I'd almost forgotten the class's bad beginning. Or at least, I'd turned it into something not so bad in my brain. This was junior high. Kids were going to do stuff. Anyway, it was just a joke. Who couldn't take a joke?

"All right," Ms. Braddy said. "Tidy up your desks, please, and Wendy, will you collect the spelling sheets?"

I shoved my book into my desk along with the blue spiral notebook I used for spelling. Crinkles of paper were caught in the wire spiral, and I poked at them with my pencil.

"Wendy?"

William snickered, and I jerked up my head. "Huh?"

Everyone cracked up. They thought I'd done it on purpose.

Ms. Braddy blinked. Her lipstick was smeary around her lips, and she looked oddly like a little kid.

"She wants you to collect the spelling sheets, *Wendy*," William said.

"Yeah, *Wendy*," said Louise. "Pay attention."

"Way to go," said Logan, smirking when I got to his desk. "You made her cry."

"I did not," I whispered. My eyes flew to the front of the room, where Ms. Braddy sat with her hands clasped in front of her. Her eyes kept blinking and blinking.

I snatched Logan's sheet and shuffled the papers into a neat stack. I placed the stack on the corner of Ms. Duncan's desk. "Um, here you go."

"Thank you," Ms. Braddy said.

"You want me to do anything else? Want me to erase the dry board?"

Ms. Braddy opened her mouth to answer, but right then the bell rang, and we watched together as everyone scrambled out of their desks and pushed toward the door. She turned to me. "Go on. I'll take care of it."

I shifted my weight. Malena was the last person out the door, and now it was just the two of us: me and Ms. Braddy.

"Go on now," she said again.

I hesitated, then walked to the door. Part of me wanted to look back, but part of me didn't.

I didn't.

During my free period—which was one *very* good thing about junior high, having a whole hour to supposedly work on homework, but which was really just for hanging out and talking—Dinah and I sat outside on a bench and discussed our Halloween strategy. Halloween itself was this

Sunday, which wasn't ideal, but was definitely doable. What stunk was when Halloween fell on a school night. But even though the actual holiday was on Sunday, our school party would be on Friday. It was going to be a daytime party, not a nighttime party, but it would be fun in its own dorky way. Music. Dancing. Sugar cookies. And of course the perfect trial run for our costumes.

"I'm going to be a cat," Dinah said.

"I know," I said. "You're always a cat."

"Because I love cats. If I had to die and be reborn as any animal, that's what I'd want to come back as."

"You'd be a very good cat," I said. "You could sleep in the sun and purr."

"What are you going to be?" she asked.

"Don't know yet," I said. "Either an angel or a devil."

"Yeah, but which?"

I shrugged. "I haven't decided."

A trio of eighth-grade guys walked past us, and we stopped talking. One of the guys, whose name was Larson—and whom I had recently developed a secret crush on—gave me a two-finger salute.

"Hey, Win," he said.

"Hey, Lars," I said back. I was glad he couldn't hear my heart, because just seeing him had made it start pounding.

They continued by, and we followed them with our eyes. Lars had such a boy walk, all slouchy-cool and pants too low, even though it was against the dress code.

"He called you Win," Dinah said when they were far enough away.

"Shh," I said, even though I knew they couldn't hear. "He's in my French class. He should be in French Two, but he's not, so he's in Ms. Beauchard's class with me."

"He called you *Win,*" she said again.

I was bright red. "Shut up, okay?"

"Does everyone call him Lars?"

"I call him Lars because he calls me Win. Now *shut up.*"

Louise walked out of Scott Hall, spotted the two of us, and strolled over. For the first time in my life, I was glad to see her.

"Hey, girls," she said. "What's up?"

"Hey, Louise," I said.

"That was hysterical in class today," she said. "Oh my God, when she called you Wendy, and you were like, 'What? What?' I about peed my pants."

Okay, so I wasn't glad to see her after all. I still felt bad about that, and I didn't want to relive it.

"Who called you Wendy?" Dinah asked.

"No one," I said, while at the same time Louise said, "The sub."

"You had a sub?" Dinah said. "Lucky." She chewed on a fingernail, one of her bad habits. "She thought your name was Wendy?"

"Yeah, because that's what Winnie told her," Louise said.

"It was a misunderstanding," I said.

"Huh," Dinah said. She wiped her finger on her jeans. "I can't see you as a Wendy. You're so much more of a Winnie."

"If we have her again, we'll have to do something even worse," Louise said. "I hope Ms. Duncan stays out all week."

And I hoped Louise would read my expression and let it go.

"Well," I said, "almost time for fourth period."

"We have ten minutes," Louise said.

"I've got to go to the bathroom," I said. "Dinah? You coming?"

Dinah stood up.

"Okay," Louise said. "Go make yourselves beautiful. But I'll see you tonight, right, Winnie?"

Oh yeah. Tonight was the night of Mom's Ladies' Guild meeting, which Louise's mom attended, too.

"I guess so," I said unenthusiastically.

"We can come up with more evil plans to get Miss Fatty." She took my spot on the bench as I got up. "See ya!"

In the bathroom, Dinah rested against the edge of the sink. "Why are you going to see Louise tonight?" she asked.

"Because our moms belong to this stupid club thing, and they drag us along." I peered at my reflection.

"Sandra and Ty, too?"

"Just me—aren't I lucky?" My eyes were a pretty shade of brown, I thought, but I wondered if they were too small. "Sandra used to come along, but now she gets out of it because of track. And Ty's a boy."

Dinah giggled. "I know Ty's a boy."

"Well, there you go." It occurred to me that maybe I should start wearing eyeliner to make my eyes look bigger. Maybe just a little, even though Dinah and Cinnamon and I had sworn we wouldn't. I wouldn't want Lars seeing me and thinking, *Oh, there's that beady-eyed girl.*

I turned to Dinah. "Hey—you could come with me tonight. Want to?"

She looked pleased at the invitation. Then she smacked her forehead with her palm. "Can't, I'm meeting Vanita. We're planning a routine for tomorrow, in case they play some Eminem."

"Going to do some lockin' and poppin'?" I asked. *Lockin'* and *poppin'* were hip-hop terms that Dinah had taught me. I couldn't do them to save my life, but Dinah could. So could Vanita, who was in the hip-hop club with her. They often got together after school to practice, and sometimes I even felt jealous.

Dinah shoved my shoulder, because she knew I was kind of teasing her. Then she leaned toward the mirror and picked at something on her chin. "Louise said 'Miss Fatty.' Is she your sub?"

"Uh-huh, only she's really Ms. Braddy."

"Is she fat?" Dinah asked.

"Maybe. A little."

"Then that's mean. You shouldn't call her that."

"I know," I said. "And I didn't. It was only Louise."

. . . .

That afternoon at Mom's meeting, I gathered with the other dragged-along daughters in the arts-and-crafts room at the community center. There was another Westminster girl there, too—a surprising and alarming addition by the name of Malena. There were also some girls from Lovett, but they clumped together and so did we.

"This is boring," Louise said to Malena and me, rooting through a cabinet. "All that's in here is yarn."

Malena read her *CosmoGirl*. She was chewing a piece of gum, pink braces and all. She'd changed out of her school clothes into a plaid miniskirt and a slim-fitting black shirt that said ROCK 'N' ROLL.

Louise closed the cabinet. She glanced covertly at Malena, and it was like I could read her mind. She was thinking, *What can I do to impress her?*

"That was great in English today, huh?" she said.

Malena turned a page.

"You know," Louise said. "With Miss Fatty."

"Omigod, her thighs were bigger than me," Malena said, keeping her eyes on her article.

"She needs support-top hose," Louise said.

"She needs a lot more than that," Malena said.

Louise's lips twitched. This was just what she wanted, for the two of them to be in cahoots. I focused on my crossword puzzle and disliked them both.

"She fell asleep in the middle of silent reading," Louise said. "Did you see?"

"*So* lame," Malena said.

"I know," Louise said. "She is the lamest substitute ever." She fidgeted with a container of glue, picking it up and digging at the dried bits around the top. "Someone needs to teach her a lesson."

Malena snorted but didn't respond. Unwilling to give up what she'd gained, Louise turned to me. "Don't you think, Winnie? That someone needs to teach her a lesson?"

"She's the teacher," I said. "She's the one who's supposed to teach *us* lessons." I meant it to come out sounding cheeky, but somehow it didn't.

Louise blew air out of her mouth. "We're stuck with her again tomorrow. I heard Ms. Lapinsky say." She put down the glue. "We should do something. Like if she falls asleep again, we should all sneak out of the room."

"Yeah, only where would we go?" Malena said.

"Well . . . then we should drop our books really loud on the floor. Or yell 'boo' right into her ear."

Malena looked unimpressed.

"No," Louise said. "No, I know. We'll tape her to the desk! And when she wakes up, she'll be like, 'Ahhhh! I can't move!'"

Malena's lips twitched. "Can you imagine? She'd freak."

Louise turned to me. I tightened my grip on my pencil.

"Winnie," she said, "go get some masking tape. I bet there's some in the supply closet."

"Ha ha ha," I said.

She sensed my weakness. "What, are you scared?"

Maybe I was. I didn't want to get the tape, but I didn't want Louise and Malena to make fun of me, either. I should have said no this morning, when Louise told me to say the wrong name. But I didn't, and somehow that complicated things. So did Malena. Her expression was bored, virtually expressionless, although I had the feeling she was keeping it that way on purpose. But there was something in her eyes that said, *Will she?*

She was so . . . worldly in her miniskirt and black shirt. She snapped her gum and folded it over, drawing it back into her mouth.

"Come on, Winnie," Louise said. "It'll be funny."

"Fine," I said. I couldn't stay there with them staring at me. "But there's not going to be any." I left the room, knowing that she and Malena were trading amused glances.

The supply closet was between the water fountain and the boys' bathroom. Its shelves were deep and wide, with enough room on the lowest one to fit far more than the one lonely ream of construction paper pushed into the back. Enough room to fit a person, even. If she crouched in tight.

Nooo, I said to myself. *Not a good idea.*

But there it was, that empty, beckoning space.

I crawled in and pulled the door shut. It was as cool and

quiet as I'd suspected. Louise and Malena could easily find me if they decided to, but for the moment—and that's all I needed, just a moment—I had escaped.

I scrunched down so that my spine lay flat against the floor of the closet and my knees grazed the shelf above. My neck was at a bad angle, but I could live with it. I knew I was being stupid and even childish, hiding there in the dark, but I needed to be alone.

I didn't like the whole "mean" kick Louise was on, even if it was to impress Malena. And it *was* mean, fantasizing about tormenting a sub. Because underneath being a sub, Ms. Braddy was a person, just like me or Malena or even Louise.

I envisioned Ms. Braddy strapped to the desk, bound firm with yards of masking tape. She would wake up, and she'd be baffled. What was going on? Why couldn't she move? She'd panic at being stuck—and then humiliation would creep in as she realized that some other teacher was going to find her that way, since surely no kid would set her free.

What if it was my aunt Lucy instead of Ms. Braddy? What if she *had* become a teacher, and some kids taped her to a desk?

I knew Louise wouldn't really do it. But what if she did?

Then came a worse thought, slippery in the dark. If I didn't stop her . . . would it be my fault?

I kicked open the closet door and scrambled to get out. I would tell Louise no, even if she and Malena made fun of me. And tomorrow, when I saw Ms. Braddy, I would admit that I really did go by "Winnie." I'd make up for the way we'd treated her.

I rose too quickly, and my head banged the shelf, knocking it free of its brackets. Art supplies rained down on me: paper, glue, and rolls and rolls of masking tape. The shelf smacked my skull, and the world went black.

The next day, Louise found me before homeroom. She bit her lip when she saw my bump, then turned it into a scowl.

"So did you end up with a concussion?" she asked. Mom had been called out of her meeting when Louise found me, dazed, in the hall of the community center, and even though I'd only passed out for a second, Mom thought it best to have me checked at the emergency room. The doctor had said I was fine, though, and that I should just take some Advil.

"No concussion," I said. "But almost."

Louise looked put out. "I wasn't really going to do it," she said. "Did you seriously think I was going to do it?"

I gazed at her, then dropped my eyes. I continued stuffing my Halloween costume into my locker.

"Not that it even matters," she said, "because Ms. Duncan came back after all. So too bad—you won't get to do any more torturing."

"I wouldn't have anyway," I said, barely out loud.

"What?" Louise asked.

The warning bell rang, followed by the sound of slamming lockers and rowdy voices as kids headed for their classrooms. Malena strolled our way with two of her buds, one of whom was Gail. They were all in Mrs. Potter's homeroom with me, and Mrs. Potter's room was right by my locker.

"Hey, girls," Louise said, trying to act as if she were one of them.

"How's your head?" Malena asked me. She and Gail and Yasmin tittered.

I shoved the last of my costume into my locker and shut the door. I took the coward's way out and pushed past without a word.

All through Mrs. Potter's announcements, I obsessed over what a wimp I was. I was the queen of wimps. I couldn't stop dwelling on it. Yesterday at the community center I'd resolved to stand up to Louise, but I hadn't, because I'd bludgeoned myself instead. Which was mortifying, so maybe I should cut myself a break on that one. But just now I'd had the perfect chance, and I'd blown it. What was wrong with me?

"Don't worry about it," Dinah told me during lunch.

"Let it go," said Cinnamon. "You're harshing my mellow."

"Huh?" said Dinah.

And then it was sixth period—time to put on our costumes. Dinah, Cinnamon, and I got ready together and *ooh*ed and *aah*ed over one another's outfits.

"You look awesome," I said to Cinnamon, who'd elected to go as a pirate. She wore a flared white shirt and tight-fitting black trousers, and an eye patch over one eye. The other eye she made up dramatically with brown eyeliner and mascara, and I said not a word even though it went against our code. I just plucked her makeup out of her bag so that I could use it as well.

"How's this?" Dinah said, twisting toward us so we could check the placement of her tail.

"Perfecto," Cinnamon said. "Girl, you look *hot*."

I did a double take. Dinah *did* look hot. She looked surprisingly curvy in her jet-black cat suit, and her cherry-red lips looked lush against her pale skin. Makeup again, I noticed.

"Whoa," I said.

"And whoa to you, too," Cinnamon said, nodding with approval at my daring (for me) attire. "You sexy thing."

"Oh please," I said. I tugged at my top, worried now that it dipped too low. Plus, the word *sexy* was just plain silly, especially applied to me.

"Shall we?" Cinnamon said, opening the door to the girls' bathroom.

"We shall," Dinah and I said together.

In the gym, a fog machine generated misty, moisty smoke, and one of those Halloween CDs offered up howls and wails. Cinnamon took off to join a group of kids doing the Time Warp, and Dinah and I migrated toward the wall.

Vanita waved from across the room in a cute pop princess outfit, and Dinah waved back.

"Check out Malena," I said, jerking my head at the refreshment table. She was dressed as a harem girl, her toned tummy on display.

Dinah sighed enviously. "You think she works out?"

"I'm pretty sure," I said.

A girl with long fake braids walked by, wearing a hoop skirt and carrying a crooked cane. One of her friends trotted behind as a sheep.

"Who's that?" Dinah said. "Is that Amanda?"

"Nuh-uh," I said. "That's Tammy Wells." I looked for Amanda, but I didn't see her anywhere. No, wait. There she was, dressed up in twinsie outfits with Gail. They were both French maids wearing actual fishnet stockings.

"Oh-oh-oh, there's Lars," Dinah said excitedly. I followed her gaze and saw him in his normal jeans and shirt.

"He looks good no matter what he wears," Dinah said.

He sure does, I thought.

Louise pranced by wearing thigh-high black boots, a black dress, and a jaunty red cap with a sequined brim. She was doing a jerky dance move that involved a lot of hipshaking, and her eyes flew from face to face to see who might be noticing.

"What's she supposed to be?" Dinah asked.

"A Brat," I said. In English we'd had to do a freewrite on our alter-identities; that's how I knew.

"A brat?" Dinah said.

"You know, as in Bratz?" I said. "Those big-headed, big-lipped doll-things?"

"Ew," Dinah said.

We watched as some teacher apparently asked Dinah's same question. "A Brat," Louise told him. Then, louder and with a frown, "A Brat, okay? I'm a *Brat*!"

"That's for darn sure," I said to Dinah.

"It's pretty sad when you have to get your fashion cues from a doll," she replied.

I laughed, and a sudden confidence enveloped me. I told Dinah I'd be back, and then I marched over to the Brat. I tapped her shoulder.

"I need to tell you something," I said.

She turned around. The song over the loudspeaker ended, and there was a big old blare of nothing.

"What?" she said.

"Uh . . ." I waited for the music to come back on. It didn't. Louise again said, "*What?*"

I lifted my chin. "You shouldn't have been mean to Ms. Braddy."

"I shouldn't have . . . omigod." She snorted. "Are you serious?"

I barreled on. "And you shouldn't have called her Miss Fatty."

The kids who could hear us snickered.

"That's all I wanted to say," I said. I marched back to Dinah as "The Monster Mash" boomed through the gym. Dinah's eyes were wide, and I knew she wanted to dish, but I put her off because a noncostumed, extremely cute boy was heading my way.

"Hey, Win," he said.

"Hey, Lars," I said. My heart thumpity-thumped. "Great costume."

"I'm Matt," he said. He jerked his thumb at one of his buddies, who was also wearing jeans and a shirt. "He's me."

"Ahhh," I said. "Clever."

"What are you?" he said, looking me up and down.

"What do you think?" I said.

He flicked one of my pointy horns. "A devil?"

"You got it."

"But a very nice devil," he said.

Oh God, had he heard me lecture Louise? Did he think I was a hopeless goody-goody?

Then I thought, *to heck with it*. He was here, and he was grinning. At me.

"Yep," I said brazenly. "On the outside I'm a devil, but on the inside I'm all angel."

November

ON THE FIFTH OF NOVEMBER, I got my period. It happened on a Saturday, just a normal old Saturday, and later it occurred to me to be glad, because what if it had happened at school? Then I would have had to tell Mrs. Potter, and maybe she wouldn't have let me go to the nurse unless I told her *why*, and nuh-uh, no way, there was no possibility of those words coming out of my mouth. I mean, what would I have said? What words would I have even used?

It was after breakfast when I felt the trickle. That was the first sign. Although I guess I was in denial, because when I went to the bathroom and saw red, I just changed underwear and threw the old pair into the laundry. In a wadded-up ball, deep at the bottom of the basket.

And then I sat very still, legs crossed, on my bed. There was something weird going on in my belly—was it a cramp? And I knew that Sandra got moody whenever she had her period. Was that why I snapped at Ty when he used too much butter on his pancakes? Oh God, was I becoming a raging mess of hormones?

I knew I should go tell Mom, but I didn't want her saying anything to me that had the word *woman* involved. As in, "Oh, Winnie, now you're a woman." She wouldn't be anything other than nice about it—I wasn't worried about that—but it was easier to sit here on my bed than to make it real by saying the actual words.

There. A pang, deep low in my abdomen. It *was* a cramp. I knew it.

And there, another trickle. Or more like a vague sensation of wetness. What if it leaked through to the bed?

I got up and returned to the bathroom, where I folded a piece of toilet paper over and over into a rectangle. I stuck it in my underwear. I flashed to a book I'd read when I was ten, called *The Thorn Birds,* where a girl my age got her period and thought she was dying of some horrible disease. *The Thorn Birds* was one of many grown-up-type books I'd read at an early age, books that normal parents wouldn't let their sweet little darling read. But Mom was like, "Sure, read whatever you want."

I'd learned a lot that way, actually. Like in *Wifey,* when the husband took pictures of his wife in her negligee, because being pregnant made her boobs turn huge. That was very enlightening. And then the wife went on to have all these affairs, and I was absolutely engrossed. I asked Mom if she'd ever had an affair, and she said, "Winnie, you can't believe everything you read in a book." And then, finger to her lip, "Not that I haven't thought about it, in the abstract.

A marriage takes hard work. You have to *choose* to stay committed."

Come to think of it, Mom was kind of inappropriate when it came to all sorts of things, not just book-reading policies. I liked the fact that she was honest with me, though.

In *The Thorn Birds* the girl cried in the bathroom and kept her bleeding to herself, until finally her mom noticed the stains and was like, "No, you fool. You're not dying. Quit whining and wash out these rags." Or something like that.

I sat back down on my bed. The toilet-paper pad felt . . . noticeable. And it was slipping out of place.

I rose and went to Mom's bathroom, where she was drying her hair.

"Just a minute, almost done," she said.

I leaned against the doorway and watched her do her thing with the round brush. Flip and release. Flip and release. So high maintenance, although I wouldn't want her looking un-flipped-and-released, I guess.

"There," she said, unplugging the cord and wrapping it around the handle of the hair dryer. "What's up?"

"You look nice," I said.

"Thanks," she said. She regarded me expectantly.

I hesitated, then blurted it out. "I got my period. I think. I'm pretty sure."

Mom's face softened. "Oh, sweetie," she said. She patted the cushioned stool she was sitting on, the one in front of her mirror. "Come here."

I walked over and scrunched in beside her. Mom put her arm around me.

"You know what this means, don't you?" she asked.

Don't say it, I prayed.

"It means you're a woman."

Aaargh.

"But what if I don't want to be?" I asked.

"All right, not a *woman* woman," she clarified. "A young woman. A beautiful young woman I am so very proud of."

I hunched my spine.

"It also means you're . . . capable of conceiving a baby. You know all about that, right?"

I was officially a thousand shades of purple. "Mo-o-om."

"All right. Okay. Just . . . keep it in mind. It's part of you now."

Enough, enough, enough, I thought. I could feel my face burning to a crisp.

Mom said, "When I got my period, my mother didn't talk to me about it at all. She just said, 'Well, go take care of it.'"

I pictured Grandmom Rosie, who made wreaths out of pinecones and who drank prune juice with her breakfast. "That's all she said? Go take care of it?"

"I don't think she knew what to say," Mom explained. "It was a different time. A different generation." She grazed my hair with her fingers. "If you ever do want to talk about any of that stuff, you can."

"I know," I said.

"Because it's likely you'll have questions. Your body is going through a lot of changes."

"I know, I know, I know."

"Okay," Mom said. "Just so you know."

"I do."

"Okay." There was a pause. Then she said, "So do you have . . . supplies? Pads, I mean?"

I looked at her in her mirror. Where would I have gotten pads? Did she think I kept a pack under my sink just in case?

Actually, that wasn't a bad idea. I would do that when I had a daughter, stock a pack under her sink. That way she wouldn't have to do the toilet-paper thing.

"Right," Mom said briskly. "You can use one of mine—as many as you need." She got up from the stool and pulled a plastic-wrapped package of Long Super Maxis with Wings from the bathroom cabinet. *With wings*. It said it right there on the wrapper.

"Here you go, baby," Mom said. She was trying not to let it be awkward, but it *was* awkward. That was just the way of it.

In the safety of my bathroom, I fitted one of the ginormous pads to my underwear. It was as big as a boat. I figured I'd be safe from spotting, though, as it came complete with reinforced four-wall protection, an antileak core, and a cottony-dry cover designed to absorb faster and help keep fluid away from my body. Good heavens, no wonder it was as big as a boat.

Product is nonflushable, the packaging also warned. Go figure.

I pulled up my jeans and checked my reflection in my full-length mirror. From the front: fine. From the back: fine again, even though it felt as though the pad was bulging out. It was enormous between my legs. It was a diaper.

I waddled to Sandra's room and told her my news.

"Yeah?" Sandra said. She swiveled her computer chair to face me. "Cool. I mean, poor you, because it pretty much sucks, but . . . cool."

I appreciated her effort to be big-sister supportive.

"Did Mom give you one of her mongo pads?" she asked.

"Uh-huh. Can you tell?"

"Don't worry. You always feel like people can tell, but usually they can't. But eventually you're going to need to switch to tampons."

"Er . . . let's not go crazy, 'kay?"

"Tampons aren't bad," Sandra said. "They're a thousand times better than pads, I promise you."

"Not today," I said. I sat gingerly on her bed. "How long do the cramps last?"

"A couple of days," Sandra said. "Mine are actually worse before my period. That's how I know it's coming."

"Oh," I said. Come to think of it, I'd been crampy yesterday, too—though I hadn't defined it as such. "How long will my period itself last?"

"Mine's five days, but everyone's different. I knew one girl who had her period for two months straight."

I paled. "You're kidding, right?"

"That probably won't happen to you, though. It was some kind of glandular disorder." She tapped her fingers together. "I read about another girl with a glandular disorder, only hers made her boobs grow to be the size of watermelons. I saw it in *People*."

"Nuh-uh."

"Yeah-huh. Can you imagine how awful that would be? I mean, you want to have *some* boobs—you don't want to be totally flat-chested—but not like that."

"What did she do?" I asked.

"The girl in *People*? She got put on some kind of drugs, but they didn't do any good. She's just going to have to live with it. Her boobs are seriously the size of watermelons—there was a picture."

I put my hand on my belly. My cramps were getting worse.

"Oh, well," Sandra said. "Like I said, it's unlikely to happen to you."

"It's so unfair," I said. "Everything about being a girl is so unfair. Why don't boys have to go through any of this?"

"Ah," Sandra said. She held up one finger, then stood and went to her bookshelf. She tugged a battered paperback free and tossed it to me. It was called *Then Again, Maybe I Won't*.

"What's this?" I said. On the cover was a boy with a pair of binoculars.

"Read it and you'll see," Sandra said. "Boys *do* have to go through stuff, just not periods and boobs."

"You mean . . ." The word *hard-on* floated into my brain,

but I wasn't prepared to speak it. I'd heard of hard-ons, but I didn't really know what they involved.

"Just read it," Sandra said. She went back to her computer. "Now go away. I want to finish IM-ing."

I took Sandra's book and waddled back to my room.

"Oh, and congratulations on being a woman!" she called out, loud enough for the entire universe to hear.

Then Again, Maybe I Won't was an eye-opener. It was as shocking as *Wifey,* if not more so, and surprise surprise, it was written by the same author, Judy Blume. She wrote embarrassing-yet-utterly-fascinating books for kids *and* grown-ups. Wowzers.

In it, a boy named Tony lived across the street from a girl named Lisa, and in the evening, sometimes, he could see her getting undressed. He knew he shouldn't watch, but he did. And he felt really guilty about it, but also really excited, and it made this crazy thing happen to his . . . boy-part. And the crazy thing that happened was called an erection.

That's what a hard-on was. An erection. The boy-part actually did get hard and, I guess, *erect.*

I imagined being a boy and getting erections, and I decided that okay, maybe that *was* as bad as getting your period. Maybe worse, because apparently it could happen anytime. And if somebody was looking, well, too bad. It wasn't something you could hide, even through your pants.

I read the rest of the novel in one long marathon sitting,

and when I finished, I was a changed person. Or woman. Whatever. And the whole experience made me grouchy.

I stomped back to Sandra's room and smacked the book down on the bed.

"Here," I said.

"That was quick," she said. She was still on the computer, because Saturdays were like that, with everybody doing their own thing. "Next you should read *Are You There, God? It's Me, Margaret.*"

"Is it by Judy Blume, too?"

"Uh-huh. It's about a girl who does all these exercises to develop her bust."

"Sheesh," I said. "Who *is* this woman? Is she obsessed with every single humiliating thing that can happen to a kid?"

"Basically, yeah." She turned toward me. "When you're older, you can read *Forever,* which is about two kids having sex for the first time."

Whoa. *Too much, too much.* And I didn't think Sandra should call it "having sex." She should call it "making love."

"I'm leaving now," I said, backing out of her room.

"'Kay, see you," she said. "Hey—have you changed your pad?"

I guess my face betrayed me, because she said, "You have to change it, Winnie. Every three to four hours, otherwise it could start to smell."

My thighs clamped involuntarily together. "Ewww! That is just *wrong*!"

"Chill," Sandra said. "It's just biology."

"It's *insane*," I said.

Sandra laughed, because she could. She wasn't the one with a yacht between her legs. "Ain't it the truth."

At school on Monday, I saw the world through Judy Blume eyes. Ms. Duncan: period. Mr. Gossett: erection. Period, period, erection, erection. Period, erection, period. I confessed to Dinah that I was turning into a pervert.

"You were already a pervert," Dinah said, giggling. I swatted her.

"You'll understand when you get *your* period," I said. "Then you won't be laughing."

"I know—that's why I'm laughing now." She squeezed my arm. "Winnie, what am I going to do when I *do* get it? Can you imagine telling something like that to my dad?"

Yikes, that's right. She'd have to tell her dad, because he'd be the only one around to tell. I hadn't thought about that.

"I'll help you," I said. "And you should, like, go ahead and get some pads now, to keep under your sink."

"You'll have to come with me," she said. "I don't know what kind to get. I don't even like going down that aisle!"

"We'll get Sandra to take us," I said. "Just be warned: she's going to try to talk you into tampons."

Dinah looked appalled. I laughed.

Cinnamon plopped down beside us on the concrete steps. She'd just come from history; her big old textbook was weighing down her backpack.

"What's up?" she asked.

I bit my lip, then leaned in close. "I got my period."

"Oh, man," she said. "You have it right now? This very second?"

"Uh-huh." I kept my legs close together, my arms wrapped around my knees.

She whistled, like *boy, that's tough.* She turned to Dinah. "Have you gotten yours?"

Dinah shook her head.

"Me neither," Cinnamon said.

"For real?" I said.

"For real. My mom didn't get hers until she was fourteen, so I'll probably be late, too."

Dinah didn't say anything, but I knew what she was thinking. She didn't know when her mom got hers.

"So what's it like?" Cinnamon asked me.

"No fun," I said. "It's like, I keep thinking it'll be gone, but it's not. Sandra says it'll last five days, so I've got two more to go."

"Does it hurt?"

"I'm pretty crampy," I admitted. "In fact, I need to go to the bathroom before next period starts."

"Next *period*," Cinnamon said. "Ha."

I got to my feet, and Cinnamon and Dinah rose with me. Wherever I went, they would go, too, and that made me so glad.

"Am I okay?" I said to Dinah. I kept walking so she could check my jeans.

"You're fine," she said.

She and Cinnamon escorted me to the bathroom, where I changed my pad and put the old one in the little trash box attached to the side of the stall. I wrapped it up in toilet paper, the way Sandra told me to. Then I flushed and came out.

"Everything good?" Cinnamon asked.

"Everything good," I said.

In the hall, kids jostled and chatted. It was a mass of humanity, everyone with their own weird and particular body. *Biology,* Sandra had said.

Out of the throng, one especially gorgeous body emerged. Lars, with his jaunty stride and messy hair. Lars, who was a boy and had . . . boy-parts. He walked beside Matt, his books tucked under his arm, joking and laughing and not yet noticing me with all the people between us.

My pulse quickened. I liked Lars—a lot. And when I talked to him, I seemed to turn into a me that was somehow not so stupid as I'd have expected. I made jokes. I acted confident. Sometimes I was witty.

Last year, I'd liked a boy named Toby Rinehart, who was really good at drawing airplanes. I thought of Toby fondly, but he went to Woodward now. He'd be drawing airplanes to impress other girls, if he still drew airplanes at all. Maybe drawing airplanes was more of a sixth-grade thing to do.

I'd thought, at one time, that maybe Toby was my Bo. But Toby was simply someone from my past, back when we were young.

Was Lars my Bo? I could see us having doughnut-eating contests, like Bo and Sandra. And Lars would watch *Oprah* with us and make smart-aleck remarks. I could see him being that kind of guy. Bo and Sandra could sit on one sofa, and Lars and I would sit on the other, and Bo and Lars would talk back to the TV while Sandra and I slugged them and told them to hush.

Stop, I told myself in my head. Just because I liked Lars didn't mean Lars liked me. I was crazy to let my mind go off like that, especially as our paths were getting nearer every second to crossing.

I pressed my spine abruptly against a locker. "Hide me," I begged.

"Why?" Dinah said. "Don't you want—"

Cinnamon yanked hard on Dinah's arm, pulling her in front of me.

"So," she said loudly, her body and Dinah's forming a shield. "Did you see the caftan thingie Mrs. Potter was wearing?"

"What caftan thingie?" Dinah said. "I was just in her class—she wasn't wearing a caftan!"

Cinnamon stepped on Dinah's toe.

"Oh!" Dinah said. "*That* caftan! The one she changed into for Dress Like a Poet Day!"

Lars passed, oblivious. I watched his jeans saunter by through a crack between Cinnamon and Dinah. He had an extremely appealing rear.

When he was officially gone, I came out of hiding.

"'Dress Like a Poet Day'?" I said.

Cinnamon giggled. We *all* giggled, even Dinah, who at first tried to maintain her composure.

"Shut up," she said. "Anyway, it's your fault. Why didn't you want Lars to see you?"

"Because of her . . . *you know*," Cinnamon said. "Right?"

"Uh-huh," I said, feeling both stupid and relieved. I didn't want to be a child, and I didn't want to be a woman, and sometimes I just didn't know how to be in between.

By Wednesday my bleeding had grown light, and it was dark brown instead of red. "Panty-liner time," Sandra told me. Panty liners were better than pads, but they were still a pain in the butt.

A pain in the *butt*. Hee hee. Cinnamon would appreciate that one.

By Thursday, my period was gone. By Friday, I actually

believed it was gone, and I wore pale blue sweatpants to celebrate. At school I resolved to plant myself in a spot where
Lars was likely to run into me, knowing that even if he
didn't, I'd for sure encounter him in French. And I'd talk to
him this time. I wouldn't hide like a scared puppy. I'd be
witty and sparkling and *normal,* and I'd put this craziness
called biology behind me.

Until next month.

December

CINNAMON HAD AN OLDER BROTHER named Carl who was a sophomore at the University of North Carolina. During Christmas break, Carl drove back to Atlanta and sold Christmas trees at Sam's Tree Lot. He lived in a trailer at the front of the lot, and he even spent his nights there, so that no one would take off with the trees.

"Who would steal a Christmas tree?" I asked Cinnamon when she was telling us all this.

"You'd be surprised," she said.

She also told us that Sam, the owner, was actually a man named Halim Palaniyappan, from India. He picked the name Sam because it sounded less ethnic.

Cinnamon and Dinah and I liked to hang out at Sam's Tree Lot after school, because it felt like a secret hideaway. Carl kept a space heater plugged into the trailer for warmth, and he had a Bunsen burner for making hot chocolate. We'd sit with our steaming mugs and breathe in the smell of pine. And we'd talk. Today, Dinah was ranting about Alex Plotkin.

"He does a *countdown*," she wailed. "It's so disgusting!

Mr. Erikson will leave the room to go get copies or some-thing, and the next thing you know Alex is back there going, 'Ten, nine, eight, seven . . .' "

"And then he *farts*?" Cinnamon said. "He can do that? On demand?"

"Apparently," Dinah said. "Then the whole class cracks up, which of course encourages him even more. I'm like, 'Could you *please* grow up?' "

"You're just embarrassed because you used to have a crush on him," I teased.

Dinah turned pink. "I did not! Winnie, you take that back this instant!"

"You did so," I said. "Don't try to deny it." I turned to Cinnamon. "He asked her to go with him, and she said yes."

"Yeah, but Winnie skated with him at our fifth-grade skat-ing party," Dinah shot back. "She asked him for girls' pick."

I couldn't believe she remembered that.

"It was under duress," I protested. "There is a very rational explanation, which is that Mrs. Jacobs asked me to. She practically *ordered* me to. I was doing an act of kindness."

"Your teacher told you who to ask for girls' pick?" Cinna-mon said.

"She felt sorry for him," I said.

"Uh-huh," said Cinnamon. She looked amused. "And you're such a good girl, you said, 'Yes, ma'am,' and did exactly what she wanted."

"Uh . . . pretty much."

"*See,*" Dinah said, as if she'd won the point.

"See what?" I countered.

Cinnamon laughed. She pushed herself up to look out the trailer window, then dropped back down.

"Any customers?" I asked.

"Just that same lady Carl's been helping for the last fifteen minutes," she said. "Buy a tree, lady. Just pick one."

Dinah grabbed a doughnut from the box we'd picked up at 7-Eleven. They were the miniature white powdered kind, and when she took a bite, her bottom lip got dusty. "Anyway, he's going by 'Critter' now."

"Who, Alex Plotkin?" I said.

"He's calling himself *Critter?*" Cinnamon said.

"He's telling people it's his nickname," Dinah said.

"Is it?" Cinnamon asked.

"No," Dinah and I said together.

"That is the stupidest thing I've ever heard," Cinnamon pronounced. She could be forceful in her opinions, and they weren't always nice. "You can't come up with your own nickname. That just brands you as a loser." She shook her head. "Why *Critter?*"

Pleased, Dinah took another bite of doughnut. She wasn't usually the one bringing stories to the table, but she'd found a treasure trove in Alex Plotkin. Or rather, Critter.

"Now Lars, on the other hand," Cinnamon said. "There's a nickname."

"Winnie made it up," Dinah boasted.

"I know," Cinnamon said.

My palms got sweaty, which they always did when Lars's name came up. But I was proud, too. "It's not something to brag about," I said. "Larson, Lars. It's pretty obvious."

"Still," Cinnamon said. She stretched up on one arm and again peeked out the window.

"What are you looking at?" I demanded. "Why are you suddenly so obsessed with Christmas-tree sales?"

She slid back down onto the pine-needle-covered floor. "Tell Dinah about today in French," she said. "When the yearbook guy came."

"Oh yeah," I said. "It was so cute. The guy was like, 'I'm supposed to take a picture of your class,' and Ms. Beauchard was all, 'These hooligans? You want a picture of these hooligans?'"

"*Hooligans,*" Cinnamon said. "She cracks me up."

"So Lars goes, 'Okay, everybody. Look like you're learning.' Then he widened his eyes and made a prissy face, like this." I folded my hands in front of me and demonstrated.

Dinah giggled. "You look constipated."

"So did he," I said. "But in a cute way."

"You think everything he does is cute," Dinah said.

"Because it is," I said.

"You need a little Lars action away from school, so that something can actually happen," Cinnamon said. Up she went, *again,* to peer out the window. This time, she caught her breath and jumped to her feet. She flashed a grin at me.

My heart did a floppy thing. "Uh, Cinnamon? Why are you smiling like that?"

A knock came at the door, and Cinnamon flung it open.

"Lars!" she said. *"Hola!"*

Every drop of my blood rushed to my toes.

"Hey," Lars said. He glanced first at Cinnamon, then at me. He was wearing a brown jacket, and it made his hazel eyes look amazing. His hair was sticky-outy, and I knew it wasn't because of gel. He was gorgeous without even trying. He was born that way.

I swallowed. "Hi," I said. *"Comment ça va?" Comment ça va* means "what's up" in French, and it sounded utterly idiotic coming out of my mouth. But it was Cinnamon's fault. She'd started it with her *hola*.

"Comme çi, comme ça," he deadpanned. *"Et toi?"*

Okay, *he* sounded good in French. He sounded good no matter what. I smiled like a big stupid smiling person.

"Sit," Cinnamon said, scooting over and patting the space between me and her. She was so naturally cool around him that it made me jealous. She was doing it for me—I knew that—but I still felt cooler on my own without her.

Lars ambled over and slouched down. His legs, in his scruffy jeans, were longer than any of ours. "So your brother sells Christmas trees," he said to Cinnamon. "Nice."

"It pays the bills," Cinnamon said.

"I'm going to make my parents buy ours here," I said.

Lame, but at least it was something. And in our mother tongue, no less.

"We'll probably pull out our hot-pink aluminum one," Lars said. "Why have a real tree if you can have a fake?"

Dinah looked aghast.

"He's joking," I said.

"Nah, we'll get a real one," he said. "One of those scrawny, pitiful ones, like in Charlie Brown."

I smiled. I loved him for referencing Charlie Brown.

We sat there, all four of us. Lars drummed his fingers on his thigh. I wished desperately that I had something scintillating to say.

Carl burst in, bringing a blast of cold air with him. His cheeks were ruddy, and he was wearing a goofy knit hat. He noticed Lars on the floor.

"Hey, man," he said.

"Hey," said Lars. He kind of saluted.

Carl turned to Cinnamon. "I need you to go make change for me," he said, handing her a wad of bills. "I'm completely out of ones."

Cinnamon stood up. "Guess I'm off to 7-Eleven."

"I'll come, too," Dinah said.

Lars and I looked at each other. Did I really want to be left alone with him? Actually, maybe that was the wrong question. Was I physically capable of being left alone with him? Not in an "oh no, better watch out" kind of way—more in a "why look, she's melted into a puddle" kind of way.

"Me, too," I said. I scrambled up. "I'm coming, too."

"You don't have to," Cinnamon said.

"I know. I want to."

"No, really," Cinnamon said. "You just stay here. You guys hang out, and we'll be right back."

"Too late, I'm already up."

"I've got to get going anyway," Lars said. He got to his feet. "See you guys around?"

"Sure," Cinnamon said. She yanked Dinah out of the trailer with her. Carl headed out as well.

Lars looked at me, then ducked his head. He kicked the floor of the trailer with the toe of his sneaker.

"You look like a horse," I blurted.

He wrinkled his forehead.

"You know. Pawing at the ground?"

"Ahhh," he said.

I got the giggles. It was all just so ridiculous.

He smiled. "Well, I'm off."

"Okay, see you."

"Yeah." He jammed his hands in his pockets. "I'll, uh, call you sometime?"

"You will?" I said. I mentally whacked my forehead. "I mean, yeah. Cool. Great. Whatever." I laughed again.

He regarded me as if I were a bit of a nut. But oh well, I was a nut—*he was going to call.*

My insides soared.

. . . .

As a family, we picked out a tree at Carl's tree lot, which was really Sam's Tree Lot, which was really Mr. Palaniyappan's tree lot. It was a nine-footer, and Dad paid twenty dollars extra for Carl to deliver it straight to the house. Which he did, with Cinnamon assisting.

"Yay!" I said when I saw her. She had pine needles sticking to her sweater, and she looked tough and woodsy as she wobbled to the door with her arms around the trunk.

"Got yer tree for ya, ma'am," she said.

I turned to the front door. "Dad? Where do you want them to put it?"

"Let's take it straight in," Dad said. He came out to take over for Cinnamon, and he and Carl shuffled the tree into the living room. Pine needles littered the floor. Dad screwed the tree stand onto the bottom of the trunk, and they slowly eased it up, with Dad doing more grunting than was necessary. When they stepped back, the top nearly touched the ceiling. Glorious, wonderful tree-smell filled the room.

"It's beautiful," I said.

"We forgot to put on the angel," Sandra said.

"Oh, man," I said. "We always do that!" Every year, we forgot to put the angel on before raising the tree, and every year, we promised ourselves we'd remember next time.

"Lift me up!" Ty said. "I'll do it!"

"You'll get scratched," Sandra said.

"I don't care."

Mom handed Ty the soft cloth angel we'd had forever, with blond hair and no eyes and droopy wings. Gold filigree stuff flaked off her dress. Dad heaved Ty up—high, high, high—and Ty arched forward and plopped the angel onto the tip. Dad set him down. Ty beamed.

"Want to stay and help us decorate?" I asked Cinnamon. The tree looked goofy with just the angel on it.

Cinnamon looked at her brother. "Can I?"

"If you want," Carl said. "But I can't pick you up till late. Like, eight o'clock."

"You can stay for dinner," I said. "Right, Mom?"

"Of course," Mom said.

Together we helped Mom unpack the ornaments. Ty and Sandra and Dad helped, too, and Dad put on a Billie Holiday CD. In a way it felt strange having Cinnamon there, because it was like, *Yep, this is our family on display. This is the way we do it, with fudge and family anecdotes and "oohs" of appreciation at the delicate paper stars that Grandmom Rosie made way back in the olden days.*

But I felt proud of us, too. I was proud of Grandmom Rosie's ornaments, which she'd given to Mom in sets of three, so that one day Sandra, Ty, and I could have one of each to start our own ornament collections. I especially liked the little wooden drummer boys with the red ribbon trim.

"Uh-oh," I said, spotting a glimmer of shiny green in the corner of one box. I dug out Jell-O, the long-legged

Christmas elf, and made it shimmy in front of Ty. "Watch out! It's Jell-O!"

"Nooo!" Ty cried, swatting Jell-O away. "I don't want him!"

"Ty's afraid of Jell-O," I explained to Cinnamon. "He thinks he's freaky."

"He *is* freaky," Cinnamon said. She took the bedraggled elf. "What's wrong with his head?"

"It's just a little loose," I said. I wedged Jell-O's plastic head back into his cloth body. Jell-O looked deranged with his pointy nose and bright red cheeks, but Christmas wouldn't be Christmas without him.

I marched over and propped Jell-O up on the tree. He wasn't really an ornament, so he didn't have a hook, but he nestled in the branches just fine. Ty waited until I went back to the sofa, then darted over and pushed Jell-O way far in so that his manic smile was hidden by pine needles. He thought I didn't notice. Foolish boy. Next ornament I put up, I'd pull Jell-O back out. This, too, was tradition.

"What does your family do for Christmas?" Mom asked Cinnamon. "Do you already have your tree?"

"We do at my dad's place, but not at my mom's," Cinnamon said. "Mom thinks it's too much of a hassle."

"Too much of a hassle?" I said. "You *have* to have a Christmas tree!"

"Not if you're Jewish," Sandra said. She was untangling a strand of lights, which was probably a waste of time because invariably our Christmas-tree lights ended up dead and broken from one year to the next. Soon she'd plug them in and say, "Great. These don't work, either."

"But Cinnamon's not Jewish," I said. "Her brother works at a Christmas-tree lot, remember?"

"Owned by a practicing Hindu," Sandra said.

"I think it's sad that your mom doesn't have a tree," I told Cinnamon.

"Yeah, it kind of sucks," Cinnamon said. Her tone was matter-of-fact. "Christmas in general kind of sucks, because first we rush through our presents at Dad's house, but we can't stay too long or it'll hurt Mom's feelings, so then we have to drive three hours to Mom's place in North Carolina. And once we get there, it's totally depressing because there's no tree and no decorations and all Mom does is bad-mouth Christina."

Christina was Cinnamon's stepmom, the one who counted the snot-marks on Cinnamon's Kleenex.

"Jesus," Sandra said. Our "happy family" routine suddenly came across in a different light.

Cinnamon shrugged. She reached for a piece of fudge, then saw it was the last piece. She hesitated, hand hovering.

"Go on," Mom said. "I've got another whole tin in the refrigerator. In fact, why don't we send some home with you when you leave?"

Cinnamon popped the fudge into her mouth. "Yum," she said. "That would be great."

Cinnamon and I didn't catch a moment alone until after all the ornaments were hung and the new lights from Dad's quick trip to Eckerd's were draped among the branches. We'd done our grand ta-da, where Sandra turned off the living-room lights at the exact second that Ty plugged in the tree, and everyone sighed in unison. Then one by one, everyone else had wandered off. Cinnamon and I stayed, slouching on the sofa amid the empty boxes. We kept the ceiling lights off and watched the Christmas tree glow.

"Thanks for hanging out," I said. "I know it must have been boring, being stuck with my family for the whole day."

"Are you kidding? I'd trade your family for mine in a heartbeat."

"No, you wouldn't."

"Want to bet?"

I smiled uncertainly, assuming it was a joke but not one hundred percent sure. Which made me aware that here was Cinnamon, a newish friend, sitting with me in the dark; in my house, away from school, with no one else to add to the mix.

With Dinah, that newness was far behind us. I always knew what she was thinking. For example, my family: she liked them, sure, but she worshiped and loved and totally adored her dad. That's why it was okay that it was just the two of them, even though it was for a sad reason.

But I guess it took a long time to know someone for real. And even then, it could all go away in a puff of smoke. Like with Amanda. Although I still *felt* like I knew her . . . until I was actually with her.

Life was complicated. But as I stared at the tree, it felt okay to think about it. My brain felt pleasantly full.

Cinnamon stretched her legs and rested her stockinged feet on the coffee table. Her toes barely reached, and she had to curl them over the edge to hold on. "So has Lars called you yet?"

I shook my head.

"Didn't he say he would?"

"Uh-huh. But maybe . . . you know."

"If he said he was going to call, he should call," she said.

"Well . . . whatever." I propped my feet next to hers. The edge of the coffee table felt cool through my socks. I got up the courage to ask something I'd been wanting to know.

"That day at the Christmas-tree lot . . ." I started.

"Yeah?"

"Do you think that Lars . . . did he . . . I mean, how exactly did he end up there?"

"Did he come to see you, you mean?" Cinnamon said. "Is that what you're asking?"

It sounded so naked out in the air like that.

"Never mind," I said.

"Yes, Winnie, Lars came to see you. I told him to."

She *told* him to? I scrunched my toes and tried not to hyperventilate.

"Why are you spazzing?" she said. "He likes you, okay?"

I was pretty much ready to evaporate and not be there anymore. But I was thrilled, too.

"Really?" I said.

She laughed. "Really."

The tree gazed at us benevolently. The lights twinkled and shone.

On Christmas morning, I ran with Ty to wake up Mom and Dad. Sandra trailed behind in her sweats and oversized T-shirt.

"It's six A.M.," she griped. "I can't believe we're up this early on a holiday."

But she was complaining for the sake of complaining. I knew she was as excited as we were.

Downstairs, we spilled the contents of our stockings onto the sofa. Along with other stuff, my stocking held a bottle of gold nail polish and a pair of silky purple underwear. Sandra got underwear, too. Hers were tiger striped.

And then came the actual presents. I got an iPod from Mom and Dad, which was super-duper cool, and a Dr Pepper shirt from Ty, because he knew Dr Pepper was my favorite drink. And because once he'd eaten my giant Dr Pepper Lip-Smacker, so he owed me. From Sandra, I got pj's from Old Navy.

It made me so happy, all the Christmas-ness in the air. I loved my family. I loved my presents. I loved everything in the whole wide world. I thought of Dinah and Cinnamon, and I hoped they were having good Christmases, too. Maybe, even though Cinnamon had to go to North Carolina, she'd have fun with Carl on the drive. They could listen to music as loud as they wanted. They could pig out on candy from their stockings.

The whole day was wonderful, but the best gift came that afternoon. I was in my bedroom making playlists on my iPod, and Ty was hanging out with me, snapping together his Bionicle.

"Winnie," Mom called. "Phone's for you."

I scrambled to pick up the portable from my bedside table, figuring it was Dinah.

"That's so weird," I said. "I was, like, right next to the phone, and I didn't even hear it ring. You think I'm going deaf?"

"Probably," said a boy's voice.

My heart hammered. "Lars?"

"Can you hear this?" he asked. He made a high-pitched squeaking sound.

"Yes," I said. I giggled. "Why are you squeaking at me?"

"Why are you telling people you're deaf?"

"I didn't say I *was* deaf. I said I *might* be. Anyway, I thought you were Dinah."

"Uh-huh, likely story."

There was a pause, just long enough for me to realize: *I'm on the phone with Lars. He called me up on purpose. He dialed my number and asked to speak to me.*

"So . . . what's up?" I said.

"Not much," he said. His tone was laid-back, as if he were settling in for a nice long conversation. "I just wanted to wish you Merry Christmas."

January

I N JANUARY, Louise had a pool party to celebrate turning thirteen. I always felt bad for people with winter birthdays, because let's face it, their party options were limited. There was Chuck E. Cheese's, back when we were five. Fit for Fun, also for when we were five. Maxine made the mistake of having a Fit for Fun party when she turned nine, and everybody sat there like, "Uh, what are we supposed to do?" Inflatable bounce-o-ramas just didn't have the appeal they once had. The thrill was gone.

With Chuck E. Cheese's and Fit for Fun off the list, there wasn't much left: the ice-skating rink, the roller-skating rink, the indoor pool. If I were Louise, I'd have just had a slumber party. But Louise wanted a pool party, probably to show off her new bikini. She told me about it the day she handed me my invitation, saying, "It is so cute. It's black and it looks like leather. It's not really leather, but that's what it looks like."

Cinnamon was standing there, too, and she whispered, "Pleather." It made me crack up.

My bathing suit was a one-piece, blue on the bottom and red and white on the top. It was very sailorish.

I was excited about the party. Not all the seventh-grade girls had been invited, and that made me feel special. But of course there was a problem, because apparently my life doesn't know how to be problem-free. If it's not one thing, it's another. Moanie-moan-moan.

I couldn't talk to Dinah about my problem, because Dinah *hadn't* been invited. And that in itself was a problem, although not as big a problem as maybe it should have been. I guess I was used to Dinah not always being invited to stuff. Anyway, Vanita hadn't been invited, either, so I told myself that she and Dinah could hang out and practice their hip-hop routines. The two of them were funny together: they had this thing where one of them would say, "Can you kick it?" And the other would reply, "You bet I can." They also said "dang" a lot. And "You *know* I'm zesty."

Once when Sandra came to the junior high to pick me up, she saw Dinah and Vanita hip-hopping in the parking lot. She watched them for a while, then said, "Dinah does know she's white, right?"

"Yes, Sandra, Dinah knows she's white," I said. "What's your problem?"

"No problem," Sandra had said. She shook her head in amazement. "Sheesh, I wish I could dance like that."

"You can," I said. "Sign up for the hip-hop club."

Sandra gave me a look, and I giggled, imagining her getting jiggy with a gaggle of seventh graders.

Sometimes I felt jealous that Dinah had another friend

besides me (not counting Cinnamon, who was friends with both of us). But for the record, I liked Vanita fine. She carried a water bottle with her everywhere, and once, after a bag of chips, she let me have a sip and didn't get all weird about the spit issue. It's just that whenever she hung out with us, she and Dinah would fall into their hip-hop riff, which left me out of the loop.

But again, my problem wasn't Dinah. My problem was that the party was today—Mom was supposed to take me in half an hour—and I'd just discovered that I'd started my period. If Louise's party was at the beach, I couldn't have gone at all, because you're never supposed to go in the ocean when it's your time of the month. Because of sharks. Mulberry Pool didn't have sharks, although it did have giant foam turtles for little kids to play on and a slide shaped like the mouth of a whale.

But, whatever. I obviously couldn't wear a pad under my bathing suit, and I obviously couldn't go without. Which left me only one alternative. It was time—deep breath—for the tampon.

Mom would be no help, so I went looking for Sandra. I found her in her room, making a pot holder on a plastic loom.

"Sandra?" I said dubiously.

"What?" Sandra said. She kept her eyes on a stretchy red band of cloth, which she wove through the other bands already in place.

"Why are you making a pot holder?" I asked.

"Because I feel like it," she said.

This was an answer, but not a very good one. "But *why*? Anyway, isn't that mine from when I was, like, eight?"

"Oh, and you're *soooo* much older now," Sandra said. "So totally beyond pot holders."

"Uh . . . yeah," I said. Like *shouldn't you be, too?*

"I found it and it reminded me of the good ol' days," Sandra said. She kept weaving. "I'm making this for Bo."

Uh-huh, I thought. *Because Bo surely needs a multicolored stretchy pot holder.*

"Okay, listen," I said, moving on to what was important. "I've got a pool party today, and I've got my period."

"So?" Sandra said.

I made an exasperated noise. "So . . . I need a tampon. And I need you to . . . you know. Tell me how to do it."

"You can take one from my bathroom," she said. "The directions are in the box."

"Directions?"

"Yes, directions, with a diagram and everything." She paused in her weaving. "That's how I figured it out, and you can, too."

I stood there. I gnawed on my thumbnail.

"What, you think I'm going to *show* you?" Sandra asked. "Gross, Winnie."

I felt myself turn red. "No, I didn't think you were going to show me," I said. But still I didn't move.

"What happened to, 'Ooo, look at me, I'm so old'?" Sandra said. Her hands were tied up with the loom, so she jerked her head toward the bathroom. "Go. I promise you, it's not that hard."

But it was.

The directions came on a folded-up piece of paper with tiny words, and the first thing I read about was Toxic Shock Syndrome and how I could die if I kept the tampon in too long or used the wrong size. *Use a tampon with the minimum absorbency needed for your menstrual flow,* the directions warned.

There was an absorbency chart on the side of the box, but it was no help. If my "flow" was less than six grams, I should use Tampax Junior. Okay, fine. But how the heck was I supposed to know how many grams my flow was? That was crazy. What was I going to do, measure it?

Anyway, Sandra's tampons were size "super," which were meant for a flow of nine to twelve grams. Again, not a lot of help there. But I guessed I'd have to go with it, since "super" was the only size I had.

I'm sssssssuper, I said to myself. *Super-dee-duper.*

I pulled out a tampon, crinkly in its white-and-green wrapper. We eyed each other.

Take a deep breath and relax, the directions said. I inhaled, then slowly let it out.

Step one. *After washing your hands, take the product out of the wrapper.* The *product?* Why didn't they call it a tampon?

I put the wrapped *product* on the sink and washed my hands. Then I picked the product back up and tore off the wrapper. Unwrapped, it looked like a mouse with a little white tail, and I remembered the time Ty stole one from Sandra's box and was playing with it when company came over.

Step two. *Get into a comfortable position. Most women either sit on the toilet with knees apart, squat slightly with knees bent, or stand with one foot on the toilet seat.* Oh, good heavens. This was way too complicated, and I hadn't even started yet, except for washing my hands. And they neglected to mention pulling down my underwear, which I assumed would have to be done. I checked the lock on the bathroom door, then pulled down my panties and sat on the toilet.

Step three. *Insert the applicator. Hold the outer insertion tube by the finger grip rings with your thumb and middle finger. With the removal string hanging down, insert the tip of the applicator into your vagina at a slight upward angle, approximately a 45 degree angle. (See image 1.)*

Whoa. Stop. My breath came in pants, because it was too many words, including the actual V-word, which evidently they could say even though they were incapable of saying "tampon." Personally, I thought "tampon" was a lot easier. Not that I was going to scream it from the rooftops or anything.

And the whole bit about a forty-five-degree angle? Yeah, right! *Um, Dad, could you please come here for a second? And bring your protractor?*

I flipped to the diagram, then immediately wished I hadn't. Noooo, no no no no. I did not like looking at that. There were two legs, and a bottom, and then swirly lima-bean shapes that I guess were the girl's insides. Her uterus, maybe? And some other organs I wasn't sure about, which in my opinion really had no business being there. And then there was the *product,* going blithely up into the depths.

This was *so* not good.

"Sandra!" I bellowed.

She didn't answer. Too absorbed in her pot holder, no doubt.

I was sweating, and I wondered if I should rewash my hands. The tampon sat limply in my palm.

Just do it, you big dummy, I told myself. *Do you want to go to Louise's party or not?*

I grimaced and wiggled the applicator into what I hoped was the right spot. Quickly I read the next direction.

Step four. *Push the tampon inside.* Oh. Well, duh. I pushed on the end of the applicator, and the inner cardboard tube slid inside the outer tube. Together, I pulled the cardboard parts out. The tampon stayed in.

Was that it? Had I done it?

I straightened my spine, still sitting on the toilet. I wrapped the applicator in toilet paper, then threw it away. The directions said it could be flushed, but that didn't seem like the best idea. What if it got stuck? What if the plumber knew it was mine?

Okay then, I said to myself. I stood and pulled up my jeans. *Well done.*

At the party, Louise wasn't the only one in a bikini. Amanda wore a bikini, and so did Gail, and so did Gail's boob-friend Malena. Malena's bikini was white with green trim, and Malena looked terrific in it. She looked like a woman instead of a girl.

Well, I was a woman, too—a young woman, anyway. I had a tampon inside of me to prove it. And who cared if I was the only one in a one-piece? One-pieces made so much more sense. There were far fewer opportunities for slippage.

"Check out the personality sponge," Cinnamon said, indicating Louise with her gaze. Louise hovered near Malena, aping Malena's gestures without even realizing it. When Malena raked her hand through her hair, Louise raked *her* hand through her hair. When Malena adjusted her bikini, Louise tugged at her own. Cinnamon made fun of Louise mercilessly, which I know wasn't very nice, especially at Louise's own party. But I'd figured out over the course of our friendship that Cinnamon had an eensy bit of a mean streak. It mainly didn't bother me, because she was never mean to me. And although she said things about other people, it was never to their faces.

"Could you be a little more obvious?" Cinnamon said. Mocking Louise, she thrust out her chest and wiggled her boobs. They bounced in her red bikini top, which she'd paired with yellow board shorts. Her tummy poofed over the top of her shorts, but I thought it was cool that she didn't care.

"Cinnamon, stop," I said, giggling.

"Why? She can't hear me," Cinnamon said. Then she dropped the act and let her posture go back to normal. "C'mon, let's go off the diving board."

I followed her to the ladder. The air smelled like chlorine, and squeals and yelps echoed off the walls. Toddlers in water wings made bright orange spots in the shallow end.

"Can you do a flip?" she asked from the board.

"Uh . . . I can try," I said.

"Just jump up high and tuck into it," she said. "It's easy. Watch."

Cinnamon sprang off the board and did a neat flip. She popped up out of the water and swam over. "Now your turn."

How hard could it be? I felt powerful there on the board, droplets glistening on my thighs. I was one of the cool people, swimming at Louise's party when it was forty degrees outside. I was aware of Amanda watching me from near the rope with the floaty things on it. She gave me a thumbs-up.

I bounced on the end of the board, then turned around and walked back to the middle. I did a three-step approach, jumped high, and flung my whole body over like I was doing a somersault. I went way too far and landed really sloppily, but I did it!

"Yeah!" Cinnamon cheered when I emerged. "Nice one!"

I grinned. Funny how trying a flip off the diving board was less scary than putting in a tampon.

"Do it again," Cinnamon said.

"Okay." I climbed up the ladder, water sluicing from my skin. As I walked to the board, I felt something between my legs. Something wrong.

Uh-oh, I thought. The Tampax box stated very clearly that if the tampon was inserted correctly, you shouldn't be able to feel it. But I could feel this for sure. Was it filling up with water? Was it expanding? What was going on?

I didn't want to go off the board. All that jouncing—not a smart idea in my current condition. But Cinnamon was waiting.

My flip this time was dreadful, worse than my first, because I didn't get nearly enough height. I swam up toward the surface of the water, and the sensation of wrongness increased. In my V-word area.

"That one kind of sucked," Cinnamon said. She laughed. "Want to try again? Third time's the charm."

"Uh . . . not right now," I said. All I could think about was my tampon. It was coming out. It was coming out right here in the pool. What in the world was I going to do?

Cinnamon wrinkled her forehead. "You all right?"

"I'm fine," I said. No way was I telling this to *anyone.* "Um . . . why don't you do one, and I'll watch?"

"Ah yes, learn from the master," she said, heaving herself out of the water.

I had only a few minutes till she was back. What was I going to *do*? A sneaky-quick feel told me that the tampon was sticking out in a way that would surely be visible if I got out of the pool. Everybody would see, even if I kept my legs clamped together. Everybody would be like, *Oh my god. Look!*

Gail's laugh rang out from the hot tub, where she and Amanda and Malena were probably analyzing each girl's body and ranking them on a scale of one to ten. Did things like this *ever* happen to Gail? Why was it always me?

The bathroom wasn't an option, since I'd have to climb out of the pool to get to it. Nor could I stay in the pool for all of eternity. Unfortunately.

Cinnamon caught my eye from the diving board, and I gave her the best smile I could muster. When she jumped, I reached up under the crotch of my suit, found the string, and yanked. The tampon brushed against my fingers, pillowy and waterlogged. I shoved it down as deep as I could, then kicked it even deeper with my foot.

"How was that?" Cinnamon said, emerging with a flick of her head.

"That was *great*," I said with too much enthusiasm. Worry panicked through me like tiny needles. "Come on, let's go to the shallow end."

"The shallow end? Why?"

I was already swimming away.

"Isn't this fun?" I said, sitting with my lower body submerged on the fish-shaped tiles. "Those kids going down the slide are so cute. I could watch them all day. Couldn't you?"

"Uh, no," Cinnamon said. She looked at me strangely. "Don't you want to dive some more?"

"You go on," I said. "I'll watch from here."

So she did. That was one thing about Cinnamon: she had no problem doing her own thing. She trotted off and joined Ansley and Sydney, and I stayed put, legs tightly crossed.

When it was time for everyone to go to the upstairs party room, I hopped out of the pool and dashed for my towel, which I wrapped snug around my hips. I didn't enjoy my cake. I couldn't have cared less about watching Louise open her presents. All I could think about was me and my leaky body and how desperately I wanted Louise's party to be over.

Please don't let anything show through, I prayed when we headed for the dressing room. I clanked open my locker and grabbed my clothes.

"Why are you putting your jeans on over your suit?" Sydney asked me.

I laughed, like *huh, would you look at that.* "Whoops!"

"Your butt's going to get wet," she pointed out.

"Oh well."

Jeans on and sweatshirt tied around my waist, I told Louise thanks for inviting me.

"I had a blast," I said.

"Don't you want to ask your mom if you can stay longer?" Louise asked. "A bunch of us are going to hang out at the snack bar."

"I wish I could, but we've got errands," I said. "Bye!"

I fast-walked out of the locker room, acutely aware of the dampness between my legs. I thought of the tampon floating somewhere in the pool, then blocked it from my mind. All I wanted was to go home.

That night, I had nightmare fantasies of the lifeguards finding my soggy tampon. What if they had some way of identifying who it belonged to? What if they fingerprinted it and connected it to me? What if they made a huge announcement and everybody found out and I got in big, big trouble?

I couldn't make my brain stop worrying about it. I tossed and squirmed in my bed, imagining them thumbtacking the tampon by its string to the pool's bulletin board. THIS IS NOT ALLOWED, the sign underneath would read. WOULD THE OWNER PLEASE REPORT TO THE FRONT DESK IMMEDIATELY.

Last summer a baby pooped in the Garden Hills pool, and they had to drain the entire thing. What if they had to drain Mulberry Pool because of me? What if they contacted Louise's parents, because we were the main teenage-ish girls there that day, and Louise said, "Ohhhh, I do remember one person who was acting kind of funny. It was Winnie Perry. She put her jeans on *on top* of her wet bathing suit. Suspicious, isn't it?"

Shut up, I told my brain. *You're being ridiculous.* Even if they did have to drain the pool, they couldn't blame it on me, could they?

I got out of bed, because I thought I'd probably go crazy if I stayed put. I padded barefoot to Sandra's room. Her lights were out, but I sat down on her bed anyway. She grunted.

"Did you finish your pot holder?" I said. I felt hostile toward that pot holder, and toward Sandra, too. She should have been instructing me in feminine hygiene instead of making pot holders for her boyfriend.

"Yes," Sandra said. "It's the most fabulous pot holder in the world. Why are you bothering me?"

I scowled. I wanted her to just *know;* I didn't want to have to tell her.

"Did something happen at the pool party?" she asked.

"Why do you say that?"

"Because. You came home in a major funk, you didn't say a word at dinner, and now you're in here bugging me when I should be getting my beauty sleep. What's your deal?"

"Fine," I said. "Be that way." I got up and stalked to the door.

"Winnie, come *back,*" Sandra said. She sighed and pushed herself to a sitting position. Grudgingly, I returned.

"So what happened?" Sandra asked.

"Nothing," I said. "But I am *not* a fan of tampons."

"Oh no. Did it come out when it wasn't supposed to?"

I nodded.

"Not . . . in the pool, did it?"

"No!" I said hotly. I burst into tears.

Sandra put her arm around me. She pulled me to her, and I pressed my forehead to her shoulder. It felt good to cry.

"You've just got to make it go in further," Sandra said. "Next time, just push it all the way in."

"There's not going to *be* a next time."

Sandra rubbed my back. She could be really nice when she wanted to be.

After a long minute, I sniffled and pulled away.

"Am I a bad person?" I asked.

"No, you're not a bad person." She looked me in the eye. "Every single female on the planet has an embarrassing period story, I guarantee you."

"Really?"

"Really. It just . . . comes with the territory."

"Oh, great."

"So go to bed and forget about it. You're still the same old you."

"Yeah, right," I said. I'd gone to Louise's party feeling like the queen of cool, and now fate and the joy of being a woman had toppled me from my throne with one quick smack. Dinah, who was uncool, was the lucky one. Far better to have stayed at home than to have left a waterlogged tampon as your personal calling card.

But my tears had washed me clean. And the next day failed to bring a squad of police cars to my door, ready to hustle me away to jail. No unidentified tampon was featured in the morning news. Louise, when I saw her Monday morning at school, treated me the same as ever. So did all the other girls.

If the tampon had been traced to me, it would have been bad. *Very* bad. And that was freaky to think about, how life could go from wonderful to terrible in the blink of an eye.

But for now, miraculously, I was safe.

February

LET'S CALL DINAH," Cinnamon said. She'd come home with me from school, and we needed something to do. We'd already pigged out on Doritos and Dr Pepper, and neither of us wanted to watch TV. Anyway, the *Oprah* that was on was one we'd already seen. It was one with Dr. Phil, who, face it, could be a little too parentish.

"Okay," I said. My eyes followed the embroidery on Cinnamon's brown hoodie. It looked like a dragon, kind of, but it wasn't a "for sure" sort of thing. What was for sure was that it was adorable. She'd paired it with jeans that she'd trimmed herself with a length of funky blue ribbon. I had total outfit envy.

"But we won't tell her that both of us are here," Cinnamon said. "I'll talk, and you listen in."

"Why?" I said.

"So that she and I can talk about you, and you can find out what she really thinks."

I must have looked shocked, because Cinnamon gave me the eyebrow quirk she reserved for when she thought I was acting young.

"Have you never done this before?" she said.

I shook my head.

"Well, it's fun. Just stay quiet—I'll do all the talking."

She grabbed the phone and punched in Dinah's number. As she did, I wondered if this was such a good idea. But I kept my mouth shut.

Cinnamon snuggled next to me on the sofa, the phone nestled between our ears.

"Hi, Dinah, it's me," Cinnamon said.

"Hi, Cinnamon," Dinah said. She sounded pleased. And far away, like a little-bitty Dinah off on her own. She'd also recognized Cinnamon's voice right away, which surprised me for some reason. I guess they talked on the phone more than I realized.

"What's up?" Cinnamon said.

"Not much, just doing my homework. What's up with you?"

They chatted about an English assignment and about Ms. Eaton's hair, and I leaned back against the cushion. So far, their conversation was completely normal. Boring, even, although there was a thrill in listening in without Dinah's knowledge. "The Secret Life of Dinah," I thought, as if it were a sitcom.

"Uh-huh," Cinnamon said. "Uh-huh." Then she nudged me with her knee. "So what about Winnie? Was she there for any of that?" Dinah had been describing a bathroom run-in with Louise, in which Louise had told Dinah that

Dinah's pants were too short. Which was true, actually.

"No, Winnie was in French," Dinah said.

"With *Lars,*" Cinnamon said. I stifled a giggle. "Do you think anything's ever going to come of that?"

"Winnie and Lars?" Dinah said. "They are so cute."

"I wish she'd go ahead and make her move, though," Cinnamon said. I opened my mouth indignantly, and she gave me a look that said, *Relax.* "I mean, it's kind of annoying how all they do is talk. Don't you think?"

"What else would they do?" Dinah asked.

Ha, I thought.

"I just think she should be more aggressive," Cinnamon said.

"I think she's doing just fine," Dinah said loyally. "Anyway, it's working, isn't it?"

"But her *clothes.* She doesn't even try to dress sexy. And what's up with those baggy T-shirts?"

Cinnamon was talking trash about me more than Dinah was, and it kind of made me laugh, but it kind of made me feel weird, too. Did she believe the things she was saying, even a little? Did she really think my shirts were too baggy? I liked baggy. Baggy made me feel safe.

"Winnie looks cute no matter what," Dinah said. "Winnie would look cute in a sack."

Cinnamon rolled her eyes. "Well, that's true," she said. I stuck my tongue out at her.

"Cinnamon," Dinah said, "do you, um . . ."

"What?"

"Do you think *I* dress sexy?"

There was such nakedness to her question that my heart went out to her. Fashion wasn't Dinah's strong point, just as apparently it wasn't mine. At least not according to Cinnamon.

"You need to get rid of your purple jeans," Cinnamon said truthfully. "But in general you look okay."

"Really?" Dinah said. "You're not just saying that? I mean, I know I'll never look as good as you and Winnie, but . . ."

"Tell you what," Cinnamon said. "Next weekend I'll come over and help you go through your stuff. We'll find some outfits that make you look fabulous."

"Yeah?" Dinah said. I could practically feel her smiling over on her end of the line. Good ol' Cinnamon, and good ol' Dinah. I was proud of being friends with them both.

At school, the Service Council was selling Valentine's Day carnations outside the cafeteria. You paid now, filled out a strip of paper with your message on it, and then the carnations were delivered to whoever they were supposed to go to on Valentine's Day morning. Cinnamon and I hovered near the foldout table, watching kids approach, scribble away, and depart. Some did it furtively. Some were bold. The Service Council was raking in oodles of cash.

"Do you think Lars is going to send you one?" Cinnamon asked.

"Hush," I said, shoving her shoulder.

"And if he *does*," she went on, "will it be pink or white?"

White meant friendship; pink meant love. Which everyone on the planet knew.

"The question is," I said, "who's going to send one to you? Maybe Alex Plotkin? Excuse me—*Critter*?"

Cinnamon shuddered. Lately Alex had taken to appearing at Cinnamon's locker reeking of Old Spice, and yesterday he'd offered her a stick of Juicy Fruit.

"Maybe he'll give you your own special countdown to delight," I said. "Three, two, one . . . kaboom!"

"Grow up," Cinnamon said, making me feel unexpectedly rebuffed. What, she could tease me, but I couldn't tease her? And Alex's fart countdown was a classic. I knew Dinah would have laughed.

Cinnamon jabbed me. "Look. Here he comes."

"Alex?" I said. "Where?"

"*Lars*. Act casual."

I spotted Lars with his buddy Bryce, and I straightened my spine. I tried to act not only casual, but sophisticated and breezy and utterly appealing at the same time. I felt strained from the effort, but that was life.

"Does he see me?" I said through my smile. Because that was the point, for Lars to see me while at the same time seeing the Service Council table, so that his mind could go *Bingo!* and he'd decide to buy me a carnation.

"I don't think so . . . wait! Yes—he definitely does!"

My cheek muscles felt rubbery. *Look pretty, look pretty*, I chanted inside my head. I'd even worn a tighter-than-usual shirt, although I don't think anybody noticed.

"There you are," said Dinah, appearing from behind us. "I've been searching everywhere!"

Her presence registered, but I didn't give her my full attention because Lars and Bryce were coming our way. I let myself glance at him as he approached—like *Oh, hi! I'm just now noticing you, just this very second!*—and he gave his patented chin jerk. Pleasure tingled through me.

Dinah grabbed my arm. "I really need to talk."

"Later," I said.

"It's about Muffet."

"Who's Muffet?" Cinnamon asked.

"My cat," Dinah said.

Lars and Bryce stopped in front of us.

"Hey," Lars said.

"Hey," I said. I couldn't help grinning.

"Winnie, it's *important*," Dinah said. "The vet said she's gaining too much weight. We have to put her on a diet, and the only treats she can have are Fishy Yum Yums!"

Bryce looked at her as if she were from another planet. "What is she talking about?" he asked Lars.

"My cat," Dinah said. "The vet says she's ten pounds overweight."

"Your cat's too fat?" Bryce said. "Dude, her cat's too fat!"

I burned a little. Dinah was the type of person who would say things like this, and guys like Bryce would make fun of her. Someone else could have said the very same thing—say, Cinnamon—and it would have been life as normal. Except that Cinnamon wouldn't have said it. I wished Dinah hadn't, either.

"It's not funny," Dinah said to Bryce. She turned to me. "You know she doesn't like Fishy Yum Yums. What am I going to do?"

"Don't give her Fishy Yum Yums," I said.

Bryce and Lars cracked up, and Dinah turned red. I hadn't meant it as a betrayal, but I could see how maybe it came across like one.

"Winnie," she said. She tugged on my sleeve.

I didn't want to go. But I didn't know how else to handle it. I felt a stab of anger at Dinah; its intensity surprised me.

"I'll see you around," I said to Lars.

"Yeah, sure," Lars said.

"Let's get some grub," Bryce said.

They headed into the cafeteria, sailing past the carnation table without a second glance.

"*Dinah,*" Cinnamon scolded. "Your cat's weight problem is more important than Winnie's love life?"

It was exactly what I was thinking. I regarded Dinah stonily.

"But she's . . . she has to eat . . ."

"Please don't bring up the Fishy Yum Yums," I said.

Dinah started to protest, and then the realization hit. Lars. The carnation table. My entire romantic future.

"Oh my gosh," she said. "I am so so so so sorry. I guess . . . I wasn't thinking?"

"Huh," Cinnamon said. "You figure?"

Dinah looked stricken, and I sighed. It was hard to be mad at her, because she never screwed up on purpose. It just came naturally.

"Winnie?" she said meekly.

I *was* mad at her, though. On the inside.

"Let's just go eat lunch," I said without making eye contact. "And you can tell us all about the Fishy Yum Yums."

At home I discovered that even Ty had a Valentine's crush. He was in crush with a girl named Lexie, who was in his kindergarten class.

"She has pretty hair," Ty told me over a root-beer float. Mom had told me to fix him a healthy after-school snack while she was out doing errands, and I figured this counted. After all, ice cream was chock-full of calcium.

"And she has pretty teeth," he said.

"Unlike Taffy?" I asked.

Ty made his face into a Taffy-style underbite, probably without even meaning to. "Unlike Taffy," he said. "But Taffy wants to marry me. I told her no, because I'm already taken."

He was five years old and he was "already taken." Where did he get this stuff?

"Well, you've got plenty of time to figure out who you're going to marry." I slurped on my float. "The main thing is to remember to be nice. Okay? You should always be nice to everyone."

"Okay," Ty said. He tilted his glass to get the melty bit. "I had a dream about Lexie. Do you want me to tell it to you?"

"Sure."

"I was at Lexie's house, and this is what happened. I made a flying jump over her—remember, this is *just* a dream—and it made her beautiful hair get messed up."

"Uh-oh."

Ty looked at me anxiously. "It was just a dream."

"I got that part. Go on."

"It did not happen in real life."

"Go *on*."

"Her hair came out of her headband, but her mom got it back how it was supposed to be. That's good, isn't it?"

I wanted to hug him. He was such a sweet, great kid. "Yes, Ty, that's very good. But you shouldn't jump over her again, 'kay?"

"It was just a dream!" Ty insisted.

"If you say so," I said.

"Win*nie*!"

The phone rang, and I got up and answered. It was Cinnamon.

"Hold on," I said to her. "Ty, you want to watch *Guts*?" *Guts* was a crazy game show for kids that I'd stumbled onto once in the upper range of our cable channels. Ty was obsessed with it.

His face lit up. "Yeah!"

"You can do that while I talk to Cinnamon. I'll come check on you in a bit."

Ty pushed his chair out from the table and scampered off.

"Hey," I said to Cinnamon. "I'm back."

"What's *Guts*?" she asked.

"Just this dumb show," I said. "Kids, like, ride giant tricycles through obstacle courses and bungee jump into pits of foam."

"Ahhhh," Cinnamon said.

"My mom hates it. But she's not here, is she?" I propped my feet on Ty's chair. "So what's up?"

"Oh my *God*," Cinnamon said. "I wanted to talk about this afternoon. At lunch."

"With Lars, you mean?"

"And Dinah. What was she thinking?"

I opened my mouth to agree, then hesitated. Cinnamon wouldn't do the listen-in thing to *me*, would she? Just to make sure, I said, "Is Dinah at your house? Is she listening in?"

"Ha ha, very funny."

"Dinah!" I called. "Are you there?"

"Winnie," Cinnamon said, "Dinah is not at my house."

"Do you swear?"

"Yes, I swear. What kind of friend do you take me for?"

"I was just checking."

"If she _was_ here, I'd have to give her a lecture on how not to be such a . . . I don't know, not such a—"

"Spaz?" I supplied.

"Ex_act_ly. What was her deal? Why was she going on and on about stupid Muffy?"

"Muffet," I said.

"With Lars _right there_. Weren't you embarrassed?"

"A little," I admitted. "I sort of wish . . ."

"What?"

"Nothing."

"_What?_" Cinnamon persisted. It was her "come on, you can tell me" voice. Cinnamon made gossiping fun, even though I knew it was bad.

"Well . . . I guess I wish she didn't act so young all the time." There, I said it. "I mean, we're in the seventh grade, you know?"

"So true," Cinnamon said.

"In my head I was like, 'Shut up already! Nobody cares about the Fishy Yum Yums!'"

"She's going to grow up to be one of those spinster ladies with five zillion cats. No one will want to go out with her because all she'll do is talk about her little darlings."

I giggled. "A cat hoarder! Her apartment will smell like cat food, and she'll have a ceramic plaque that says PURRRR-FECT hanging in her kitchen."

"You know I love Dinah," Cinnamon said. "But I do wish she'd clue in a little. Like, there's a time and a place for everything."

"And today wasn't the time or place for any of it," I said. It felt liberating to get it all out. "Bryce didn't want her there, Lars didn't want her there, and I sure didn't want her there. How could she not know?"

A choked cry came over the line, and then Dinah's trembling voice. "Maybe because no one ever told me—until now!" Then a click. My heart literally and truly froze in my chest.

"D-D-Dinah?" I stammered.

"She hung up," Cinnamon said, sounding amused.

"But . . . you said . . ."

"I said she wasn't at my *house*. You didn't ask about three-way."

A sick feeling spread over me. I sat there, clutching the phone.

"Winnie?" Cinnamon said.

I made no sound.

"Oh, relax. You didn't say anything *that* bad."

But I had. In Dinah's mind, and in my own, I knew I had.

"I'll call her back," Cinnamon said. "It was a joke, okay?" Her tone was exasperated, but with an underlying thread of worry, too. She shouldn't have done what she did. *I* shouldn't have said what I did.

She grew brisk. "I'm hanging up now, Winnie. I'm saying good-bye. So take a chill pill—everything's going to be fine."

. . . .

But it wasn't. The next day at school, Dinah refused to talk to me. As in, nada. Zilch. Not a single "hello" or "bug off" or even "I hate your guts."

"Dinah, please," I said when I caught her between classes. "I didn't know you were on the line!"

She opened her locker, her lips pressed together.

"Don't be this way," I said. I tried to angle myself in front of her. "I'm sorry, okay?"

She shut her locker with a clank. She strode down the hall.

"Dinah!"

She didn't turn around.

Cinnamon said she was being a baby. Dinah wasn't talking to her, either, but Cinnamon shrugged it off, saying, "Her loss." I was furious at Cinnamon, but I didn't know what to do with my anger. I didn't want to lose *both* my friends. Although right now, Cinnamon didn't even feel like a friend. Not only because she'd played the phone trick on me, but because now that she had, there was all this weird space between us. Maybe because she felt guilty? But she wouldn't say that out loud. Instead she just acted as if I was being stupid.

In English, Louise said, "I hear Dinah's giving you the silent treatment. What gives?"

"I don't want to talk about it," I said.

Louise stared at me. There was something hungry about her curiosity.

"Well, she's being completely immature," she said, and I felt ridiculously close to crying. Ten to one, she'd say the same thing to Dinah the second I wasn't around. I hated the fact that other people—*Louise*—knew our personal business.

It turned out Lars knew, too. He came up to me after French and asked if I was okay. I was slumped at my desk, staring off into space, and I guess I looked pretty pathetic.

"Not really," I said.

"How come?" he said. "I mean, is it because of your friend? Dinah?"

I lifted my head. His hazel eyes gazed down at me, and part of me was aware that I could take this and milk it, making Dinah the bad guy and me the innocent victim. And then Lars could comfort me, and it would be a way of getting closer.

But I was too torn up to make that happen.

"I did something mean," I said miserably. "But not on purpose."

"If it wasn't on purpose, then why is it such a big deal?"

"Because it *is*. Because now she won't talk to me."

"She's stonewalling you?" He frowned. "Man, why do girls do that? Why are they always making such big deals out of stuff?"

"I don't know," I said.

"It's stupid."

I knew he was trying to help, but he wasn't.

"Have you never gotten into a fight with Bryce?" I asked.

Lars shrugged. "If Bryce gets on my nerves, I tell him to lay off."

I stared at my fingertips, at the dry skin around my nails.

"Just tell her you're sorry," he said.

"I did," I said.

Kids filed in for next period, and Lars shifted his weight.

"Well . . . see ya," he said.

I curved my mouth into the best smile-shape I could, but I could feel that it wasn't working. "See ya."

Sandra, when I filled her in on the situation, said the same thing Cinnamon had said to me outside the cafeteria, before all the bad stuff happened.

"You bad-mouthed your best friend?" Sandra exclaimed. "God, Winnie. Grow up."

Grow up, grow up, grow up. Couldn't everyone see that I was trying? I blinked back the tears that had popped up out of nowhere, and Sandra softened.

"She won't give you the cold shoulder forever," she said. "Just suck it up and tell her you're sorry, you idiot."

"I have!" I cried. "A thousand trillion times!"

"Then tell her again," Sandra said, like *duh*.

But when I rang Dinah's house, her message machine answered.

"Dinah, are you there?" I said. "I'm sorry, okay? I'm so so sorry! *Please* call me back!"

She didn't. And for the entire next day, she continued to

shut me out. She wouldn't look at me. She wouldn't talk to me. Between math and history, when I normally saw her in the hall, Vanita ushered her past me with her arm around her shoulders. Dinah kept her head down, and Vanita glared at me with disdain. It made me feel sick with shame. Worse than that, it made me feel . . . scared. Heart-racing, shallow-breathing scared. As if everything I knew about myself had been jerked out from under me. As if I'd been standing on firm ground, and then—*whoosh*! Suddenly I went sprawling.

The weekend came and went with no word from Dinah. In my room, I played a hip-hop CD she'd made for me, over and over. It was a way of feeling close to her, even though there was this one song, "Never Too Late," that absolutely shattered me. It was about best friends and worst friends, and how "a worst friend is just a best friend who's done you wrong."

Which I guess meant that I was both: best friend *and* worst friend. Or best friend turned into worst friend. The song's chorus tried to make everything okay, saying you could always pick up the phone and apologize. But I *did* pick up the phone. I called Dinah fifteen times before I gave up. She was probably with Vanita. They were probably talking about what a witch-with-a-B I was. I imagined the two of them together, maybe eating olives out of a jar, which Dinah loved and I found disgusting. A hole opened inside me like nothing I'd felt before.

"It's because you're used to being the more popular one,"

Sandra said, finding me huddled in the darkened TV room. I wasn't even watching a show.

"What are you talking about?" I said. "I'm not more popular."

"Don't be coy," Sandra said. She sat beside me on the sofa, and her weight made me tip. "You're, like, the one with power. With best friends, there's always one who's cooler or prettier or whatever. And that's you."

"That's a terrible thing to say," I said. My mind flashed to Amanda, back in fifth grade when *we* were best friends. In that case, she was the one with power.

"But now Dinah's grown a spine," Sandra went on. "And you can't handle it."

My eyes burned. It was those dumb tears that kept brimming up out of nowhere.

"It's true, isn't it?" Sandra said.

I saw it now: it *was* true. I needed Dinah to be uncool, so that I could be cooler. And then I went and made fun of her for it, and I was called out. And now she was friends with Vanita instead.

"I'm an awful human being," I said.

"Pretty much," Sandra said.

A sob broke out of me, and she relented. She put her arm around me and pulled me close. The darkness outside had deepened, and I shut my eyes and pressed my face against her shirt. I tried to keep my crying sounds to myself.

"She'll come around," Sandra said. "Just next time, treat her the way she deserves."

"I will," I whispered. *Oh please, please, please. I will.*

Monday was Valentine's Day. That meant carnations. I got one white carnation from Cinnamon and one white carnation from Dinah, which she'd no doubt ordered before I called her a cat hoarder that no one wanted around. I held it tight and blinked. Stupid tears.

I also got a pink carnation from Lars, which *did* give me a stab of pleasure even though I was so sad. Receiving a pink carnation was a badge of honor. I glanced around at the other girls in my homeroom. Did Gail get a pink carnation? No, she did not. Did Malena? Well, yes, actually. She got four. But, whatever. At least I got one.

"Who's it from?" Ansley asked, gesturing at my flower.

"Um . . . Lars," I said.

"Larson Colman? Isn't he an eighth grader?"

I nodded.

"Why aren't you squealing your head off? I would be."

What was I supposed to say? Because I don't have any squeals left?

The end-of-homeroom bell rang, and my stomach cramped. In a few moments I'd see Dinah by our lockers, and her expression would tell me if she liked me again or not. I knew better than to hope she did—but I *did* hope it, nonetheless. I would always hope that. For the rest of my life if I had to.

Anyway, I'd done something special to show her how sorry I was. Yesterday I'd gone to Richard's Variety Store and picked out what I wanted, and this morning I'd arrived at school early and hunted down Eve Smith, the seventh-grade Service Council rep. Eve had been dubious, but finally she agreed to deliver it with the Valentine's carnations.

I filed into the hall with everyone else. I saw Dinah exiting Ms. M's room. My blood moved thickly through my veins.

She scanned the hall. That was a good sign, wasn't it? I lifted my hand halfway in a wave, then changed my mind and drew my thumbnail to my mouth.

She saw me, then turned abruptly and fiddled with her lock. I hurried over before she could do something crazy, like go to class.

"Thanks for the carnation," I said in a rush. I was just going to pretend she'd meant it, because at one point she had.

She wrapped her arms around her chest. In one fist she clutched three white carnations. I saw nothing in the other.

"Dinah . . ." I said. My voice cracked. "Are you going to hate me forever? Please just talk to me! *Please!*"

And then, unexplainably, *her* eyes welled up. "Fine," she said. "Talk."

Relief gushed through me. I felt weak.

"I was a bad friend, and I'm sorry," I said. "I don't know why I said those things. I was just caught up in the moment, and—no. That's an excuse. I mean, it's true, but—"

"You could have just *told* me," Dinah said. Her voice was as shaky as mine. "If you think I'm so spazzy, and that I shouldn't talk about Muffet, why didn't you *tell* me?"

Her question stopped me cold. Why hadn't I? If I always kept those thoughts inside, how was she supposed to know?

"I just . . ." I said. "I guess I never . . ."

She looked at me, blinking hard. It was real, what was passing between us, and so raw that I wanted to look away. But I didn't let myself. I wasn't allowed.

"I never planned on ignoring you," Dinah said. "It just . . . happened. And then I didn't know how to stop!"

"I don't care. I don't care about anything as long as you forgive me." I grabbed her hand. "Dinah . . . I *do* want you around, okay?"

"I know," she said. "I want you around, too."

"So you're not best friends with Vanita now?"

She looked surprised, like it would have never occurred to her to think such a thing. "I'm friends with Vanita, but not *best* friends. I'm best friends with *you*."

I grinned, and it quivered at the edges, and I could feel that it was *this* close to one of those sobbing grimaces that take over your face and make it cave in. But I was ecstatic that she liked me again. It was huge and glorious inside me.

"But, Winnie?" Dinah said. She fished around in her backpack. "Why did you give me a King Kong saltshaker?" She pulled it out. It was made of shiny black ceramic, and around its neck was the strip of paper I'd attached, just like the ones on the stems of the carnations. *I'm ape over you!* it said. *Your best friend, Winnie.*

Seeing it in Dinah's hand, I felt confused about why I *had* given it to her. It seemed, well, ridiculous in the bright light of the hall.

"Winnie?" Dinah prodded.

"Um . . . because they didn't have any Beanie Babies?" I said. "Well, they had puppies and bunnies and a duck, but I wanted to get you a kitten. But they didn't have any. So I got you him instead."

King Kong regarded us. His eyes were dark and shiny.

"I thought it would be funny," I said sheepishly.

Dinah started to laugh.

So did I.

"Let's go show Cinnamon," she said.

"Okay."

The bell rang for first period, and we stopped in our tracks.

"Oh yeah," I said. "Class."

"Oh yeah," said Dinah. "Well, afterward?"

"It's a plan."

She made King Kong wave. I waved back with my carnations.

She spotted my pink one, and her eyes grew wide. "Is that from Lars?"

I nodded.

"Winnie, that's awesome!"

"I know," I said, because it was.

March

O N THE FIRST DAY OF MARCH I woke up with a something-special-is-going-to-happen feeling, like on Christmas or Halloween. For a minute I couldn't figure out why, and then it came to me: it was my birthday month. We'd officially reached my birthday month. I wouldn't turn thirteen for eleven more days, but that was okay. In fact it was preferable, as it gave everyone time to plan all sorts of birthday secrets. Under my covers, I wiggled my toes.

It was a school day, which meant I'd be seeing Lars, so eventually I forced myself to get up and make myself look presentable. I wore my favorite jeans, which were hand-me-downs from Sandra. They were beat-up old Levi's, and their rips and worn spots were real, not made by some jean-ripping machine. I paired them with a gray T-shirt with a single hot-pink star, and I finished the look with my flower earrings, the ones I got when I first pierced my ears. It seemed so long ago.

I analyzed myself in the mirror. I looked pretty good, I had to admit.

I turned sideways. Before long I was going to need a new bra, maybe even a B cup instead of an A. Yikes.

At the breakfast table, I broached the topic of my party.

"So, you know it's March now," I announced.

"Omigod, she's learned her months!" Sandra said. "She's a genius!"

I ignored her. Mom pressed the microwave POWER button to heat up our sausage-and-biscuits.

"I was thinking maybe something small," I said. "For my party."

"Small is good," Mom said. "Ty: chocolate milk or orange juice?"

"Chocolate milk," Ty said. "With lots of chocolate-y."

"Just Dinah and Cinnamon, and they could spend the night, okay?"

"I thought Cinnamon was on your bad list," Sandra said.

"*No,*" I said indignantly. Cinnamon and I had never talked about it, the whole three-way telephone debacle, but since then she'd said some things that showed she was sorry. Like once during lunch, she'd said, "I don't know why you guys even put up with me. I am such a dork." And another time she'd said, "Just don't listen to anything I say, all right?"

Maybe I should have told her outright that what she did was mean. That I was mad at her for it—or at least, that I *had* been mad. But I didn't really know how to tell people that stuff, and anyway, by now things were pretty much smoothed over. Although the incident was something to file away in my brain under the heading of "Cinnamon."

The microwave beeped. Mom popped it open and distributed our biscuits.

"So can I?" I asked. "Have a sleepover with Dinah and Cinnamon?"

"I suppose," Mom said.

"And can you take us to the mall?"

"I thought you hated the mall," Sandra said.

I groaned. I knew she was purposely trying to be annoying.

"FYI, I'm going to be a teenager," I explained.

"So?"

"*So*. Teenagers go to the mall."

"Oh, good Lord," Sandra said.

"Ty, what are you doing?" Mom said. The biscuit part of his sausage-and-biscuit was full of holes, and crumbs littered the table.

"I'm drilling tunnels," he said. "It's what Cody and I do in the sandbox."

"No more tunnels," Mom said. "Eat."

"We call it Tunnel Town."

"You can make Tunnel Town in the sandbox, not in your breakfast."

"And at the mall, we want to get makeovers, okay?" I said.

"I don't know," Mom said. "You look beautiful just the way you are."

Yeah, yeah, yeah. Mothers always said that. "I know, but just to see. Please?"

Mom looked at me. I smiled.

"I'll think about it," she said.

"Okay," I said happily. In Mom language, "I'll think about it" meant "yes."

I wolfed down my biscuit, eager to get to school so I could tell Dinah and Cinnamon. It was shaping up to be a very good birthday.

"Wow," Dinah said. "I mean . . . wow. You're going to be a teenager."

"So are you, eventually," I said. We were sitting on the bench outside the junior high, enjoying our last few moments of freedom before the bell rang to signify the end of lunch.

Cinnamon cleared her throat. "Already am," she said, waving her hand like, *ahem, let's not forget about me.*

But Cinnamon had seemed like a teenager from the day I first met her, even though at that point she hadn't been. So there was nothing weird about her being thirteen.

Me, on the other hand.

I kicked my feet against the ground. In less than two weeks, I'd say "thirteen" to the question of how old I was. On forms and stuff, "thirteen" was what I'd write. It sounded so much older than twelve—and I wasn't making that up. It did. I felt sorry for Dinah, knowing that she had five more months to go.

"Who's going to do our makeovers?" Dinah asked, referring to our spectacular shopping-mall plans. "They won't put on *too* much, will they?"

"They won't," I assured her. Although really, I had no idea.

"You can tell them what sort of look you're after," Cinnamon said. "Natural, sophisticated, evening . . . whatever."

"I'll say 'natural,'" Dinah said.

"What's 'evening'?" I asked.

"For a night on the town," Cinnamon said. "When you want to look really glam."

"Ahhh," I said.

"That's what you should pick," Cinnamon said to me. "And then afterward, we should hunt down Lars. And you should kiss him." She grinned. "That would be your birthday present!"

I blushed. "Ha ha."

"I'm so serious," Cinnamon said. "It's high time you made your move. Isn't it, Dinah?"

Dinah giggled.

"Shut up," I said. "If you didn't happen to notice, we're at school? With thousands of people all around?"

"Where?" Cinnamon said. The only people in sight were a couple of high-school kids, cutting across the quad.

"Well, there *could* be," I said.

"You're going to have to kiss him sometime, so you might as well do it on your birthday," Cinnamon said.

"When you're glam," Dinah added.

"I am going to have to hit both of you if you don't be quiet," I said. Even my scalp was burning. "*Please.*"

The bell rang, and the kids who'd been lingering in the cafeteria came streaming out. Voices rang out as they headed for our building.

"Look at that, time to go," I said. I hopped to my feet.

Cinnamon stood up with me. "You're such a wimp," she said. "But we know you'll do the right thing when the time comes."

"*When* the time comes," I said. "Operative word: *when.*"

"But you *are* going to kiss him?" Dinah exclaimed. "Oh my gosh!"

I quickly backpedaled. "*If* the time comes! *If!*"

Cinnamon laughed. "Too late, you said it!"

But instead of torturing me any more, she mercifully changed the subject. "Hey, let's go to Lenox this afternoon and scope out the different makeup counters, so we can choose who we want to do our makeovers."

Dinah's brow furrowed, then cleared. "I can. I don't have piano, because Mrs. Schneider's sick."

"I'm sure I can, too," I said. "Maybe we can get Sandra to drive us."

"Let's meet at pickup," Cinnamon said. We did a group

handshake to seal the deal, and I thought how lucky I was to have them, even when they teased me. Or maybe especially when they teased me, because it made me feel so loved.

When school let out, I grabbed my books and went to the sidewalk by the junior-high parking lot. Kids lounged by the wall, waiting for their rides, and a row of moms in station wagons snaked along the asphalt. I scanned the line: no Sandra. But I'd tracked her down during her free period, and she'd said yes about taking us to the mall. Then I'd called Mom from the school phone and told her not to worry about coming to get me.

There was something bugging me in my shoe, so I pulled it off and shook it. A pebble flew out. I hopped on one foot as I tugged my sneaker back on, then lost my balance and nearly fell on my butt.

Someone caught me.

It was Lars.

"Whoa there, Bessie," he said. His hands gripped my shoulders, and he eased me back into a standing position.

"Thanks," I said, feeling myself—as always—turning red. Would I ever have a moment with him where I *didn't* turn red for one reason or another? He probably thought this was my natural color. He probably called me "tomato girl" in his head.

But his hands, his strong beautiful hands. On me. It was worth being a klutz if this was the reward.

Lars dropped his backpack and lowered himself to the concrete stairs so that he was sitting at my feet. The sun shone on his face as he squinted up at me, making his eyes look almost translucent.

"So what's up?" he asked.

"Nothing," I said.

"Want company?"

"Well . . . I'm waiting for Dinah and Cinnamon. We're going to the mall."

He hesitated a fraction of a second, then said, "Oh. Cool."

I could have kicked myself. *I'm waiting for Dinah and Cinnamon* sounded like *No, I don't want company*, which was as far from the truth as you could get.

"But they're not here yet," I said, dropping down next to him on the step. Our jeans practically touched, that's how close we were. I thought about what Cinnamon had said, the whole "you should kiss him" business, then willed the idea from my brain. What if he could sense it? What if he could read my mind?

"What's going on at the mall?" he said. "Going to throw some pennies into the fountain and make a wish?"

"Maybe," I said, even though I knew he was kidding. "I loved doing that when I was a little kid."

"Me, too."

"Actually, I still do."

He laughed. "Me, too."

I could imagine him with all the toddlers, thrusting his

fist in the air and going "Yes!" when his penny landed in the highest, trickiest spot.

He shifted, and I felt a feathery warmth on my fingers. Him. His skin. Our hands next to each other on the concrete step, pinkies touching. Did he know it? Did he feel the energy sparking between us, like I did?

I edged my hand closer, and his slid over mine and closed around it, just like that. I could hardly breathe.

"*There* you are," Cinnamon said, appearing from behind. Dinah followed after. "I've been calling and calling, but you were lost in your own little world."

Panic rose up, and my instinct was to jerk my hand free. But Lars squeezed tight.

"*Ohhh,*" Cinnamon said, noticing.

"What?" Dinah said. Then *she* noticed. Her eyes widened, and I was afraid she was going to faint right then and there. Or if she didn't, I would.

"I was waiting for you guys, and Lars just happened to come by," I stammered.

"So I see," Cinnamon said.

"Um . . . yeah."

Lars grinned at me, and even though I was embarrassed, I was really really happy, too.

We held on.

Turn the page
for a preview of the next novel
featuring Winnie . . .

Thirteen

March

THE THING ABOUT BIRTHDAYS, especially if you just
that very day turned thirteen, is that you should know
in your heart of hearts that the world is your oyster. Even
if you don't like oysters, because of the slime factor. And
because they're gray. And have no eyes. Eating an oyster is
like swallowing a fishy blob of Jell-O, and frankly, I'm not a
fan. I would not, however, run away shrieking if someone
dangled an oyster in front of me, like my bff, Dinah, would.

Last year on my birthday, I snuck home a shrimp from
Benihana, because in addition to being anti-oyster, Dinah
is also possessed of a shrimp phobia, the poor dear. I waited
until just the right moment, then whipped out the shrimp
and jiggled it in front of her, making scary shrimp *I'm-going-
to-get-you* noises. There was shrieking. There was cat fur.
There was an extremely irate older sister—that would be
Sandra—who huffed off with her tub of shrimp-juice-tainted
mud mask, which Dinah and I had kind of borrowed.

Ah, the good ol' days.

But today was a good day, too, because today I turned
thirteen. It was big, and that bigness hummed inside me

even though I tried to play it cool when first Mom and Dad, and then my friends at school, made the obligatory "Ooo, a teenager at last" sort of comments. Dorky, dorky, dorky.

And yet, there's truth behind the dorkiness. I will never be a "child" again. People might call me a child. In fact, I'm sure they will, and I'll glare at them hormonally. But my childhood days are over. There's a Bible verse Grandmom Perry made me learn . . . what was it? *When I was a child, I spoke as a child, I understood as a child, I thought as a child. But now that I am grown, I have put away such childish things.*

It has a tinge of sadness to it, despite the glory of my slumber-party-to-come, complete with Bobbi Brown makeovers at the mall. Growing up is always tinged with sadness; that's what I was coming to learn. You got boobs, but you also got zits. You got to wear cooler clothes, but you felt self-conscious when people noticed you in them. You realized your parents weren't perfect and amazing and all-powerful, which was liberating in a way, but, well, you also realized your parents weren't perfect and amazing and all-powerful. Which sucked. As a little kid, I thought my parents had all the answers. As I got older, I realized no one did.

And let's not forget the friend thing. Back in the olden days, it was all so easy. Take my little brother, Ty, for example. He's six, and he's friends with everyone, even the kids he doesn't like. I went with Mom to pick him up from school last week (because Westminster, where I went, had a teacher work day, and Trinity, Ty's elementary school, didn't), and I saw this kid reach over and pinch Ty on his side. The kid laughed after he did it, and not in a nice way.

"Who was that who pinched you?" I asked him after he climbed into the backseat.

"Gary," Ty said.

"*Why* did he pinch you?"

"Because he has sharp fingernails. And because he wants me to think he's a snake, because I'm scared of snakes."

"What a jerk," I said.

"Winnie," Mom warned.

"Fine, he was *acting* like a jerk," I said. Mom was okay with that, with our saying that someone was *acting* jerky or stupid or annoying. She just didn't want us saying someone *was* a jerk. My opinion was that Mom was *acting* naïve to think that made any difference. "Anyway, a snake bite wouldn't feel like a pinch."

"What would it feel like?" Ty asked.

"I don't know. Not a pinch."

"A stabbing pain of hot lava?"

"And it wouldn't be on your waist, either, unless the snake slithered up your pants."

"Winnie!" Mom said.

"It wouldn't," I said. "And I don't like Gary for doing that."

"Me neither," Ty said. "He should go to the juvenile detention center."

"So maybe you should stand in the pick-up line with someone else," I suggested. "One of your friends, and not Gary."

Ty had looked puzzled, though he'd just two seconds earlier agreed that Gary was a bad seed.

"Gary *is* my friend," he said, as if he were explaining some basic fact.

In seventh grade, if someone pinched you hard enough to bring tears to your eyes, you wouldn't stay friends with them. Only instead of pinching, a seventh grader was more likely to be snake-like in other ways, like whispering to someone that you were "trying too hard" if you wore pink eye shadow. Or that your shirt was too tight. Or too loose. Or that you really needed to clip your toenails if you didn't want to gross everybody out.

So as a seventh grader, no, you weren't friends with people you didn't like. But sometimes you also weren't friends with people you *did* like, which was complicated, and which didn't make sense if you tried to explain it. Sometimes things just changed. That's where the sadness came in.

I can't really complain, though. Dinah is my BFF number one; Cinnamon is my BFF number two. Plenty of people have more than one best-friend-forevers. That's allowed. And my ex-BFF is Amanda.

On the very extremely plus side of being thirteen, I also have a—yikes!—plain old BF, as in boyfriend. *Maybe*. I mean, I don't want to be all braggy about it, because it's not as if he rented a billboard and painted "I LOVE WINNIE" across it for all the world to see. And please, we are *not* to the love stage. Nonie, nonie, no.

But he did hold my hand, tee hee. He held my hand for the first and only time last Thursday, and it was glorious. Plus he's absolutely gorgeous, with his hazel eyes and slouchy-boy saunter and messy, adorable hair. He jokes around with me, and sometimes I feel almost normal with him, and I definitely have the thought that I could be even more normal around him one day, with practice and mental pep-talks and *shoulders back, stomach in* reminders. And then, far off in the future, we can get married and watch TV together and have billions of little Larses and Winnies.

No! Ack! Where did *that* come from?

Please don't let Lars have received that as a weird psychic message through the stratosphere, I begged the world. Sometimes, even though I knew it was impossible, I feared my innermost thoughts *could* be heard. Not just by God, but by unintended recipients like my dead grandfather and a certain hazel-eyed boy.

Just kidding! I thought loudly. *Not planning on marriage, at least not for a long, long time! Not that desperate and girly!*

It did unnerve me, liking Lars and having him (yes, just admit it) like me back. That was a big part of why I had so much to be thankful for, on this day of becoming a teenager. And when I said that a thirteen-year-old should have the world as her oyster, what I meant was this: I hope my life will be this good forever. I hope my life will always be a secret pearl, shimmery and full of promise.

Thirteen-year-olds are too old to blow out candles (though I know I will anyway), but that's my birthday wish.

Dinah's dad pulled into our driveway at five, and Cinnamon's dad followed right on his heels. Or wheels, rather. Dinah and Cinnamon both live with their dads: Dinah because her mom died way back when she was a baby, and Cinnamon because her parents are divorced. Her mom lives in North Carolina, a three hour drive from Atlanta. Cinnamon has a stepmom, but it isn't a great thing. Her stepmom puts people down a lot, including Cinnamon.

Cinnamon's dad is cool, though. He's a hotshot Atlanta developer who has big-time clients, and sometimes he gets us tickets to random concerts.

Cinnamon hopped out of her father's Lexus and ran up the driveway, past Dinah who was still saying "bye" to her dad. I bounced on my toes on the front porch.

"Happy birthday, you birthday-having fool!" Cinnamon cried, giving me a big ol' hug.

I grinned. "Thanks."

Dinah kissed her dad's cheek in the front seat of their station wagon. They were very close, in a totally sweet way, and I was glad for both of them, because I think you'd need that if someone you love died. She climbed out, got her overnight bag from the backseat, and came to join us. She and

Cinnamon were going to spend the night even though it was a Sunday—so cool! We squealed and did a group-hug-spazzy-thing. We were like jumping elephants.

"Party time!" Cinnamon said.

I helped the two of them lug their stuff inside, then called out to Mom.

"We're ready!" I said. "It's time to go! Our personal beautician awaits!"

"Not beautician," Cinnamon said. "Beauticians are frumpy old ladies who went to beauty school."

"With big hair," Dinah contributed.

"Our personal makeup consultant awaits," Cinnamon said.

"*Riiight*," I said, like *thank you, O Wise One*.

Mom clopped downstairs in her heels and a snazzy pants-and-blouse combo. She wore such *Mom* clothes, tailored and put-together. Even when she wore jeans, they were crisp and dark blue and high-waisted, with her shirts tucked in according to the law for forty-year-olds. She was cute in her little outfits.

"Hi, girls," she said.

"Hi, Mrs. Perry," Dinah and Cinnamon chorused.

"So let's do it," she said, because she still thought she was hip. To Dad—who showed up in the kitchen to see us off—she said, "See you on the flip side, homie."

"Oh dear god," I said, as Dinah and Cinnamon giggled. "Mom? Do not *ever* say that again."

Mom laughed. "Tell me not to say something, and that's exactly what I'll greet you with the next time I pick you up from school. *And* I'll be wearing clown shoes."

"Have fun, girls," Dad said, ruffling my hair and then Dinah's and then Cinnamon's. "Just don't go too crazy!"

At Lenox, Mom told the woman behind the Bobbi Brown counter at Neiman Marcus that we were "only" thirteen (which wasn't even true, Dinah was still twelve) and to please give us a look that was "appropriate." Then she gave me her credit card, said we could all pick one product to buy, and went off to check out the sales rack in the women's department.

"Okay, this is going to be fun," the Bobbi Brown lady said as soon as Mom was out of earshot. She was Asian, with gorgeous pale skin and dark eye makeup. I guessed she was in her late twenties. "My name's Aimee, and I say let's just go for it. What do you think?"

"I think I like Aimee very much," Cinnamon said under her breath.

"Winnie first, because she's the birthday girl," Dinah said.

"No, I want to go last," I said. I was excited about being made over, because I myself was crappy with makeup, and so pretty much avoided it like the plague. And it seemed so naked and embarrassing to have it on your face, visible to the world in a way that said, "Hey, look! I care about being pretty!"

Except I *do* care about being pretty. *Dor* I don't think there's a single person in the world who doesn't care about being pretty. Any female, at any rate.

Well . . . backtrack, backtrack, backtrack. I *used* to not care what I looked like. On a scale of one to ten, my appearance scored about a "two" in terms of importance. One more weirdness of getting older: appearance now ranks way higher, like even an eight or nine.

But I didn't want to be the first to get made over, because I'd been struck with a sudden case of the jitters. The naked thing again.

"Do me," Cinnamon said. She hiked herself onto the stool. "I want smoldering, baby." She growled. "I am a tigress!"

"You got it," Aimee said.

She smoothed moisturizer over Cinnamon's skin to provide "a good base" and explained that Cinnamon didn't need foundation. "None of you girls do," she said. "Enjoy it while you can."

She stroked green eye shadow over Cinnamon's lids, which she said Cinnamon could pull off because of her green eyes, and used a black eyeliner around her eyes. "But only from the middle of the iris out," she said. "You don't want your eyes looking squinched together."

Cinnamon blinked at Aimee's touch, although she was clearly trying to hold still. The eyeliner made Cinnamon's eyes "pop," to use Aimee's expression.

She finished the look with jet black mascara and something called a "color brick" on Cinnamon's cheeks. It was a cool shimmery blush that was a mix of three different pinks.

"Ta-da," she said, twirling the stool so that Cinnamon faced us like a painting.

Dinah drew in her breath. "You are so gorgeous!" she said.

"Yeah?" Cinnamon said.

"You look terrific," I said. She did, in a striking, daring, club-girl way that was perfect for her. It was a look I could never pull off. It just wasn't me. "You look so old!"

Cinnamon hopped off the stool and picked up a hand held mirror. "Aw, man, I *love* it," she told Aimee. "And I already know I want that color brick thing for sure. Or maybe the eye shadow!"

"Would you wear the eye shadow to school?" I asked.

"Yes," Cinnamon said, like, *Of course, why wouldn't I?*

"Your turn," Aimee said to Dinah. She patted the stool. "Hop on up here, sweetie."

That made Cinnamon and me laugh. *Sweetie.*

Dinah blushed. Out of all of us, she had the absolute least experience with makeup, because of having no mom or step-mom or older sisters. And because, even though she was twelve, she didn't always act it. When it came to makeup and boys and stuff like that, she acted more eleven-ish, or maybe even ten.

Like how she was wiggling backward onto the stool, adjusting her bottom by lifting up one cheek and then the other. When it was my turn, I'd do a quick, confident hop, like Cinnamon had. I wouldn't adjust my bottom.

"Let's see," Aimee said, tilting her head to study Dinah's features. Dinah held her smile in a way that showed she knew she was being scrutinized. Round face, white skin, blue eyes—that was Dinah. My little kitty-cat girl, *so* not a tigress. Which was as it should be. In a threesome of friends, there isn't room for more than one tigress.

Aimee got to work with something called "Moon Glow," which she said would "add radiance" to Dinah's skin. "It has reflective particles that catch the light and bounce it back," she explained. "Angelina Jolie uses it."

Dinah giggled. She jutted her chin forward to meet Aimee's touch.

Aimee stroked on a smoky eye shadow and lightly lined Dinah's blue eyes with gray eyeliner. I noted how she did it, with lots of small dashes rather than one continuous line. She used a tiny brush to paint Dinah's lips with a deep cherry stain.

"There," she said. "What do you think?"

Dinah looked in the mirror. Cinnamon and I leaned over her shoulders.

"Whoa," Cinnamon said when she got her words back. As for me, I remained speechless. Dinah looked . . . beautiful. How had Aimee done that? Was it the cherry-red lips? Or maybe it was the Moon Glow. Dinah's skin was luminescent.

"Oh my gosh," Dinah said. She put down the mirror and grabbed a Kleenex, rubbing at her lips.

"What are you doing? Leave it!" Cinnamon said.

"It's too red!" Dinah said. "I look like a . . . like a street walker!"

Aimee laughed. "Sweetie, you do *not* look like a street walker."

She kept scrubbing. "I do!"

"Dinah, stop," Cinnamon said. She grabbed Dinah's hand. "You're not used to it, that's all."

I wasn't used to it, either. I was confused by what I was feeling, which I recognized by its prickly claws in my stomach.

"Honest, you look fabulous," I said, trying to push the jealousy away. Jealousy was stupid and wrong, especially when it came to Dinah. I should be happy she looked so great! I was happy. I *was*.

"Anyway, it's just for fun," I said. "Nobody says you have to make yourself up every day."

"You've got to get that lip stain," Cinnamon said. "That has to be your one thing."

"Well, don't *force* her." I laughed. "Dinah, it's totally up to you."

She got off the stool, easing herself down until her feet touched the floor. It was downright weird seeing this beautiful Dinah. I couldn't get over it.

Aimee patted the stool to say it was my turn.